From the tower window, I see a still and flat land before me, an empty desert of baked earth and small scrub brushes flattened by wind. The sky is overcast, the reddish clouds above are thick and heavy. It is not sunset or sunrise, but the reflection of heat and flame. Part of the city beneath me is on fire and I suspect that whatever we have wrought has gone terribly wrong.

The tower is massive, soaring into the sky above the city like a gigantic arm thrust toward the heavens. It is made of clay bricks that mirror the dull color of the plains below. Behind me is a small, square worktable. I turn my attention back to my duties.

A mirror above the table catches the light and I see that my linen shift is stained with soot and something else . . . blood. The symbols stitched into it, that mirror those on the Board set upon the table, are unmarked. The magic that preserves them still holds. I glance at my face in the mirror, and my tired eyes stare back at me. There is a flash of power in them and I know I can continue.

I must continue.

D A U G H T E R **OF** D E S T I N Y

KEEPER
OF THE
winds

JENNA SOLITAIRE

TOR

A TOM DOHERTY ASSOCIATES BOOK
NEW YORK

KEEPER OF THE WINDS

A Tor Teen Book
Published by Tom Doherty Associates, LLC
175 Fifth Avenue
New York, NY 10010

www.tor.com

Tor® is a registered trademark of Tom Doherty Associates, LLC.

Library of congress Cataloging-in-Publication Data

Solitaire, Jenna.
    Keeper of the winds / Jenna Solitaire.
        p. cm.—(Daughter of destiny; 1)
    Summary: After the death of her last known relative, Jenna discovers a mysterious board in her attic and learns from Simon, who works for the Vatican, that she is a "Keeper," with powers and a destiny inherited from her grandmother.
ISBN 0-765-35357-1
EAN 978-0-765-35357-3
[1. Supernatural—Fiction. 2. Winds—Fiction. 3. Adventure and adventurers—Fiction. 4. Antiquities—Fiction.] I. Title.

PZ7.S6892Kef 2006
[Fic]—dc22

                                                                    2005053794

First Tor Teen edition: February 2006

Printed in the United States of America

0 9 8 7 6 5 4 3 2 1

This first part of my story is dedicated to every girl or woman out there who has ever felt alone and yet found the strength to carry on, even in the face of certain defeat.
You all have my admiration.
—Jenna Solitaire

PROLOGUE

"I can't let them have it!"

My voice is a bare whisper, a faint gasp in the dark, stone stairwell. I follow the cold steps down, spiraling along the wall of the castle. Inside, voices rise and fall in sudden alarm, echoing around me. They know I am gone. They know I have taken the Board.

I'm almost running now, my long white gown tangling in my feet, making me stumble as I flee. An ache stabs my side as I pant for breath, but I clutch my treasure tighter to my chest and keep moving. If I can find a door, a way outside, I can escape. The winter night, the thin crescent of the moon, will hide me.

Faster down the stairs, brushing cobwebs away from my face, and faster still, until I see the faint outline of a door at the bottom of the steps.

I grasp the iron handle and shove with all my might until the door opens, letting a blast of cold air wash over me. My hair whips across my face, long red tresses loose in the winds that swirl around the castle. The winds have been blowing for days, ever since I arrived here with my father. The man who betrayed me and gave me, and the Board, to them. From that sin, there can be no redemption, and the rumors I have heard that the Mother Church is calling him to a reckoning will only be the beginning of his tragic end. Of that, I am certain.

My body is chilled, yet I am sweating. My breath comes in painful gasps, yet I am strangely exhilarated by the chase, by the possibility of freedom and having the Board to myself.

Behind me, I hear excited voices growing louder, echoing down the stairs. The knights have found the secret passage I used to escape my room. They are coming—and this time, I know they will take the Board from me, tearing it from my broken fingers if they must.

I leave the shelter of the castle, ignoring the icy sting of snow on my bare feet. Running again, the winds swirling around me, my gown in a white billow snapping like a sail, my hair a red, angry cloud around my head. As I reach the wall surrounding the courtyard, I call upon the Board, and it answers. Its voice is a familiar, sibilant whisper in my mind, yet its power is in every syllable. It knows what I desire before I can even articulate the thought. The wind strengthens again, twisting like a tornado, wrapping around me and putting me in the center of a vortex. The force of it levitates me up and over the twenty-foot high stone barrier between myself and freedom.

I hear my father's voice cry out a name. Elisabeth.

My name? I do not recognize it. Is it my name he calls or someone else's? His voice sounds strange to me. As if he's not the same man who used to sit me upon his lap and sing songs during Yuletide. It matters not. All that matters are the winds dancing around me now, protecting the Board and myself and ensuring our escape.

The island we are on is small and the harbor is near. I smell the salt of the ocean and hear the waves whispering like icy razors against the rocky shore. The voices following me grow distant as they try to find my trail. The winds carry their words away. The Board knows me, knows my wants and needs, and the winds wrap around me in a protective cloak, holding me up and carrying me toward the sea. I do not believe the Board will lead me to harm, though I have only the smallest knowledge of its powers.

Something is wrong, though I do not know what it is. The sky is a dark green, almost emerald, and the clouds are boiling. Stars flicker in the distance. The Board is somehow both hot and cold in my arms. The winds carry me closer to the water. That is where I will escape. The Board tells me that they must think I am dead, never to look for me again. I do not have a plan, but know that if I listen to the Board, it will save me.

Looking down, I see a stone pier, jutting out into the night-black water. Without warning, the winds cease. I drop into *the dark waters beyond the pier like a stone. I do not have time to breathe. I clutch the Board, my skin pricked by a thousand icy needles.*

I am afraid.

I am not afraid.

I try to swim, but my gown is waterlogged and encumbers me almost as much as holding on to the Board does. No matter what, I must hold on to the Board.

Sinking faster, the water rushes past me. Into my nose, my mouth. I want to breathe, scream, the pain in my limbs stabbing like knives. I cannot stop myself.

I inhale; the cold rush of water fills my lungs.

The sensation is both terrible and wonderful. It burns deep inside me.

The Board is slipping from my hands. I can't let it go. I must not let it go.

And that is when I scream, "I can't . . ."

But my voice is nothing, silenced by water, and all I see are the muted bubbles of my desperate words rising to the midnight surface of the windswept harbor.

"Forgive me, my Lord—"

"I trust you have an excellent reason for disturbing me at this unholy hour?"

"We have found a lead. This obituary was located in the website archives for an Ohio newspaper."

"Solitaire? The Margaret Solitaire?"

"The same, my Lord."

"Get your team to this . . . Miller's Crossing . . . immediately. You know what to do."

"I can't let it go!"

The words were torn from my throat in a gasping scream. I shot out of bed and the blankets that entangled my legs flew everywhere. The images had seemed so real. It felt like I was drowning, my lungs filling up with the dark waters of my dream.

I took a few steadying breaths, feeling sweat cool on my aching forehead. I had always been plagued by bad dreams, vivid and filled with powerful winds and storms, but I usually

5

knew I was dreaming. This one had felt more like an out-of-body experience, like it had really been happening to me.

A sudden blast of air was followed by the heavy splatter of raindrops on my window. Dim light filtered through the curtains, and I tried once more to grasp my dream—but a sense of wind and water and a cold castle filled with angry knights were the only images that came to me.

Outside, the early spring sky was gray and fog hovered close to the ground. *Perfect weather for a funeral,* I thought. A glance at my bedside clock told me that if the sun were going to burn off the mist, it would have done so by now.

Today, regardless of the poor weather, I would bury my last known relative. My grandfather. The man who raised me, and who had always been my source of comfort when the dreams had woken me screaming in the night. Now he was gone. And with the exception of my few friends, I was alone in the world. *A perfect fit for my name. Jenna Solitaire. Jenna Alone.*

I grabbed my robe and shoved my arms into the patterned sleeves. I couldn't afford to feel sorry for myself right now. Sighing, I headed downstairs to brew coffee before I had to face the day and the first of many decisions that I would be making on my own. Wisdom, I realized as I went down the steps, was one of many qualities I would miss about my grandfather.

"From dust we came and to dust we return. Yet no one is ever truly gone. Lord, we ask that you help us to find comfort in knowing that our good friend Michael McKay is not gone either. He is lost to our sight, but not our hearts, and one day we will all be reunited in the kingdom of Heaven."

Father Andrew's words were supposed to be comforting, but I felt like my life had taken a sharp left turn into the surreal. Everything moved in slow motion, and it felt like I'd been in a trance from the moment I'd found my grandfather slumped over in his favorite chair—dead of a heart attack that had come without any warning signs at all. Ever since, it had felt like I'd been walking under water.

I shuddered, the thought of being under water bringing back the last moments of my dream. Even the headstones around us reminded me of it: the granite was the same greenish-gray as the pier stones had been. The small cemetery behind St. Anne's church, where I had gone to Mass every Sunday growing up, looked even more gray and dreary in the rain. The church itself wasn't a gigantic Gothic cathedral in the true Catholic tradition. It was a large brick building, plain and unpretentious. The most striking features were the stained glass windows over the door and along the walls, surrounding the area where the congregation would sit during Mass, and the garden that was planted in the sheltered corner between the church and the rectory.

Father Andrew had fallen silent, and I suddenly realized that he was looking at me. The mourners—friends of my grandfather's, for the most part—were all staring at me, too.

"Oh," I whispered. "Sorry." I stepped forward and laid a white rose on the casket. Others followed behind me, leav ing flowers as well. Old Mrs. Bronson, one of our neighbors, left a yellow carnation, pausing to kiss a small, golden crucifix around her neck before moving on. Dale Harkins, the Realtor who owned the house behind ours, stopped and crossed himself briefly. Several more people my grandfather had known—friends and neighbors and even occasional acquaintances—passed through the line, offering a flower or a silent prayer for his soul.

As I watched the mourners file past, I felt the weight of someone's gaze, and glanced around the cemetery. A well-dressed man on the far side of the access road matched my stare. I didn't recognize him, but then again, I didn't know all of my grandfather's friends. Still, the man stared at me so intently that I wondered if he knew *me*, but before I could place him or figure out what he was doing there, I heard Father Andrew clear his throat quietly.

He gave me a subtle nod, and I moved to stand next to the coffin as it was lowered into the ground. It was early spring, and the open grave looked like a raw, gaping wound. The rich, loamy smell of the disturbed earth made my empty stomach roil. The coffin settled into place with a thud that I felt in the pit of my stomach. And in my heart.

"Heavenly Father, we send you our friend Michael McKay and ask that you receive him. Comfort those left behind with your presence and with the knowledge that in your realm, there is only peace. Amen," Father Andrew concluded. He gave me a final nod, his thinning blond hair stirred by the wind, and his blue eyes magnified by the round lenses of his glasses.

I bent down and picked up a clod of cold soil from the mound next to the grave. Unshed tears stung my eyes as I crumbled the dirt in my hand, slowly letting it fall onto the coffin. The sound it made as the dirt settled in the flowers on top of the casket made a strange harmony with the rain that drizzled onto the tented roof overhead.

I stepped away from the grave, and as tradition dictated, the mourners all lined up quietly, waiting to say a few words to me that were supposed to be comforting.

"I'm so sorry for your loss, Jenna," Mrs. Bronson said. Up close, I saw that her black dress had tiny, almost invisible little white flowers patterned on it. It seemed disturbingly out of place at a funeral, as though deep down, she were celebrating her ability to outlive yet another person.

"He loved you very much, Jenna." This from Dale Harkins who'd at least had the grace to dress properly in a sober black suit and blue paisley tie. He offered his hand and I shook it. "If there's anything I can do?" he said, his voice so low I almost missed it.

"No," I said. "Thank you. I'll be fine."

He nodded and moved away.

I continued to thank people, when all I really wanted to do was cry. Or at least ask them to shut up—there were far more empty platitudes about death than I'd ever realized. My best friend Tom Anderson, and his girlfriend, Kristen Evers, had also come. They waited until almost everyone else had offered their condolences before coming forward. Tom and I had been friends since grade school, and he didn't speak, didn't offer a platitude, but simply stepped forward and wrapped me in his arms. He was taller than I was, and though he was a computer nerd to the core, he had a lanky frame that was surprisingly strong. My grandfather had said he had "whipcord muscles."

He practically lifted me off my feet and just held me. After a few moments, he stroked my hair and whispered in my ear: "You loved him very much, Jenna, so it's okay to cry."

And then I did.

I hated making a spectacle of myself, but I knew I was. The sobs shook my body and all I could manage to do was bury my head in his shoulder and wait for the storm to pass. A memory of my grandfather telling me long ago that the Solitaire women never cry in public passed through my mind. I felt Tom stroking my hair, and Kristen patting me gently on the shoulder.

Finally, as my tears started to subside, he let me out of his embrace. "Better?" he asked.

I nodded, sniffled, and managed a weak, "Yes."

"This will help, too," Kristen said. She handed me a shard of quartz crystal shot through with amethyst. "It's a healing crystal. I got it at the Rainbow Cauldron Connection and the lady there said it was sure to make you feel like a new woman . . ." Her voice trailed off and she paused, turned to

Tom, then added, "Or was it sure to make you feel *up* a new woman?"

She said it in such a serious tone that for a moment, I didn't realize she was joking. Kristen was a sweet-natured girl who believed in absolutely *everything*, including the story she often told about being abducted by aliens at the local Holiday Inn. Her voice was what I tended to think of as "softly lost in space." She smiled at me, and I couldn't help myself. I started to laugh. "Oh, Kristen, what are we going to do with you?" I asked, crying and laughing and trying my best not to snort all at the same time.

"You can buy *me* a crystal sometime," she said.

"Done," I replied. "But after I've gotten through all this."

She nodded. Kristen and I weren't close, but she handled the friendship between Tom and me very well, never saying a word even though anyone with eyes could see he wanted more from me. I didn't, and was just happy to have them both as friends.

"I'm glad you came," I said to them. "It means a lot to me."

Tom nodded, and said, "That's what friends are for."

"You're welcome," Kristen said, pulling on her gray gloves and smoothing out the sleeves of her wool jacket. She looked around the dreary scene, her blonde hair pulled back in a tight ponytail that glistened with raindrops. "If it's any consolation, your grandfather has *got* to be in a better place than this one, anyway."

I was forced to agree. Miller's Crossing, Ohio, was never

going to be more than a wide spot in the road with a small college and an even smaller mall. "Yes, I'm sure he is," I said.

"I've got to get to work," Tom said. "They'll kill me if I miss another shift, but I can come by later if you want."

"I'll be fine," I said. "I'm just glad you could be here today."

"You're sure?" he asked.

I gave him another hug, and nodded. "Yes, I'm sure. I think I want to be alone for a little while, you know?"

"I understand," he said. He took Kristen's arm. "Ready?"

"Yes," she said in her soft voice. "I've never been fond of cemeteries. All those wandering memories." She shuddered and I chose not to ask what she meant. Kristen was a strange girl in a lot of ways.

"Try to take it easy today," Tom said, and then they wandered off toward her car. The last few mourners passed by, offering condolences. I knew only a handful of them by name, and that was a testament to how many people had known my grandfather. As the last of them left, I moved back toward my grandfather's grave. I wanted to say one last good-bye.

Thinking I should say something to Father Andrew, I turned to look for him and noticed the well-dressed stranger again. The man wore a long black topcoat that draped him perfectly, and his hands were sheathed in skin-tight black leather gloves. His entire outfit screamed "expensive." He stood next to a large memorial statue and was pointing something in my direction. A cell phone? It took a second for me to realize that he was using the built-in digital camera to take pictures. I didn't know who he was, but my already frayed nerves snapped.

"Hey!" I shouted. "Hey you!"

People turned to stare, first at me, then at the stranger. His dark hair was perfectly styled, even in the rain, and was touched with silver at the temples.

"What do you think you're doing?" I yelled, moving toward him.

The man turned and walked away, but before I could chase him down and find out what he was doing, Father Andrew grasped my arm. "Easy, Jenna," he said.

I took a deep breath. "Do you know that guy?"

Father Andrew shook his head. "No, I don't," he said in his quiet voice. "But I've seen his type before."

"His type?"

"Some people are fascinated by funerals," he explained. "They generally don't mean any harm."

I thought of the stranger's dark stare, his hooded gaze, and shivered. "I don't think he was here because he's fascinated by funerals," I said. "He was staring at me like he knew me."

Father Andrew turned and looked in the direction the man had gone. "It's not worth chasing after him, Jenna. I think you've had enough strain for one day."

I looked at where the workmen were leaning on their shovels, waiting for everyone to leave so they could fill in my grandfather's grave. Nodding, I said, "You're right, Father. It's time to go."

He escorted me past the garden toward my car. "I'll drop

in and check on you," he said, his voice gentle. "Just in case you need anything."

I paused as we passed the garden, smiling at memories of my grandmother's way with plants and flowers. It had been her inspiration and sweat that had made the church gardens at St. Anne's so beautiful. Her gravestone, etched with MARGARET MCKAY SOLITAIRE, BELOVED WIFE AND FRIEND, was right next to my grandfather's. She had died when I was just eight, only a few years after the car accident that had claimed my parents' lives.

Nothing had bloomed there yet, and the flowerbeds had been covered with straw for the winter. The grass alongside the brick paved path looked brown, wet and sad. The statue of Mary gazed down on the empty ground as though she wondered where all the color and brightness in the world had gone.

For the last eleven years, my grandfather had been my only family. Absently I reached up and touched the silver medallion hanging around my neck. I had taken it from my grandmother's jewelry box that morning and put it on before the funeral, thinking it might somehow make me feel more connected to my family. There were letters engraved on it, the initials *M* and *M*—*M* for *Michael* and *M* for *Margaret*. On the back, another *M* had been added when their only daughter, my mother Moira, was born.

Father Andrew wasn't the first person to offer to come by. It was like everyone in town thought I was still eight years old and incapable of caring for myself. Still, this was the man who had baptized me, guided me through my catechisms, and given me my first communion. He was also a friend of my grandfather's, and had known my grandmother when she was alive, too. I offered him a tired smile, all I was capable of at the moment. "I'd like that," I said, knowing it would please him.

"Good enough, then," he said. "I'll see you tomorrow." He walked me the rest of the way to my car, and shut the door after I got in, waving to me as I drove away.

The dreary day, the dark-eyed stranger taking my picture, my grandfather's funeral, and the disconcerting dream all made for a long ride home to an empty house.

The afternoon stayed as gray and miserable as the morning, and the phone wouldn't stop ringing. Father Andrew had suggested that I have a reception after the service, but I'd decided not to. Most of the people who would come would be friends of my grandfather's, not mine, and while I appreciated the condolences, mostly I wanted time to myself. My plan had been to clean the house—immerse myself in the mundane—but what I'd ended up doing was wandering from room to room, losing myself in memories.

I had known that people would be calling, but I hadn't quite expected the flood of calls I'd been receiving, and had almost resolved to take the phone off the hook when it rang again.

"You have a great burden to bear," a male voice said. The tone was deep and held a hint of an accent I couldn't identify.

"Who is this?" I asked.

"That is not your concern. Your concern now—your only concern—must be the protection of the Board."

I could almost hear the capital *B* in his words.

"The Board?" I asked. "What are you talking about?" When the caller remained silent, I said, "Who *is* this?" I could feel my knuckles aching from my tight grip on the phone and I had to consciously relax my hand.

"We will speak again," he said, and the line went dead. *Perfect,* I thought. *Now I've got a phone freak to add to my day.* I punched star 69 on the keypad, but the number was blocked.

As tempted as I was to unplug the phone at that point, I couldn't. If I didn't answer, people really would worry and then I'd have a houseful of visitors. I'd taken the last few days off from school and had a research paper to work on that was due by Monday—funeral or no funeral. I looked at my books stacked on the kitchen table and knew that reading or studying was, at least for the moment, out of the question. I wanted to tackle cleaning the attic the next day, but it seemed like nothing really appealed to me as a way of taking my mind off my grandfather's death.

Which left what exactly?

"Not very much," I said. For a moment, I could almost hear my grandfather's voice saying, *"Jenna girl, talking to yourself again? Do you answer yourself, too?"* I smiled at the memory, and then realized that I would never hear him chide me about this habit again.

I brewed a fresh pot of coffee, poured a steaming cup, and then wandered over to stare out the rain-streaked window into the backyard. The downpour had slowed to a steady drizzle, and the grass held only the faintest undertones of green. Hints of spring, my grandmother would have said.

Once again, I could almost hear my grandfather's voice chiding me. *"Jenna, my girl, always face reality. The truth will sometimes hurt, but it will never hurt as much as a lie. Especially one you tell to yourself."* I'd been lying to myself for the last few days, trying to find reasons why I wasn't alone. But the truth was that my family was gone. I *was* alone.

Finally, I decided to just go to bed. Even my dreams had to be better than this aimlessness, and tomorrow, I could face the task of sorting through my family's old belongings in the attic.

Perhaps that would help me get on with the rest of my life, or at least put some of my past behind me.

My dreams that night were more chaotic than usual, with violent winds and strange images of faces and symbols I didn't recognize. Thankfully, the dream of drowning I'd had the night before hadn't repeated itself. The next morning, I woke and felt a little better.

"More real anyway," I muttered to myself while checking my backlogged e-mail. Outside, the weather remained gray and damp, with occasional gusts of a chill wind, though the rain had finally stopped.

The most important note I saw came from Tom.

```
Dear J.—I hope you got some rest and are
maybe feeling a little bit better today. I
know you need a friend right now more than
you want to admit, so call me later, okay?
I'm here for you whenever you need me.—T.
```

I sent a quick reply, promising to call him later. He was sweet and a good friend.

I dressed in my oldest jeans, tied my hair back and climbed the rickety, creaking steps to the attic. The house wasn't exceptionally old, but it *felt* old to me—perhaps because it had been my grandfather's house for as long as I could remember and I associated him with it. The steps leading to the attic were the pull-down kind, with a runner of green indoor-outdoor carpeting going up the center.

My grandfather had left the house and everything else to me, but I planned to sell most of it to add to the nest egg that had been growing in the bank since my parents had died. Between the sale of the house, my grandfather's life insurance, and other money I had saved, I would be able to finish college without working a job or taking out student loans that I'd have to spend the rest of my life paying off.

I knew it was the smart thing to do, as Mr. Eiger, my

grandfather's lawyer said, but in truth, it broke my heart to get rid of the house. It was the last tie I really had to my family. I had grown up here. It was a home filled with memories.

The attic was dark, lit only by two small windows at either end and a bare bulb hanging overhead. The attic was a repository for anything my grandparents couldn't get rid of at their twice-yearly yard sales. I remembered my grandfather teasing my grandmother that she couldn't resist buying the old junk at *other* peoples' yard sales. She would store broken appliances, musty books, and old records here briefly before breaking down and letting my grandfather sell it all off again. It was an endless cycle. I smiled at the memory of their mock arguments.

I hadn't been up here since my grandmother had died. Some of the dozens of stacked boxes were open, and a few were even labeled. I opened the topmost box, coughing as dust flew into the air. It looked as though my grandfather had saved every school project I ever brought home: terrible paintings with blurry stick figure images, animals made out of construction paper, spelling tests with WOW! or GOOD JOB! stickers on them. A warm sense of being loved passed through me—that they had saved all of this memorabilia from my childhood said so much about them as good people trying to be good parents. I also felt more than a little sad knowing they were both gone now.

I found a box containing old scrapbooks, and I pulled one out at random and flipped through the pages. My sixth birthday party, when Billy Shoemaker from next door threw my cake on the floor during a tantrum. First communion. My sweet sixteen party, when Billy Shoemaker snapped my bra strap as I went to blow out the candles on the cake, and I turned around and gave him a black eye for his trouble. High school prom, which I attended sans Billy Shoemaker. Graduation. A lot of memories, and my grandfather had been there for all of them.

I was sad that he was gone, but so happy that he'd been a part of my life, too.

Next to a box of dusty Christmas ornaments, I spied an old black trunk with tarnished brass fittings and latch. The lid was open. Inside were a whole bunch of black-and-white photographs. I reached inside for a handful. Men in old-fashioned suits, women in skirts from another age. A pretty woman with a wide smile laughed at the camera from beneath a lacy white veil. It took a moment for me to realize that she was my mother on her wedding day.

I traced my fingertips over the image—my mother's long, red hair that was a half-shade darker than mine, her green eyes that looked like cloudy emeralds, the heart-shaped curve of her jaw . . . I couldn't remember her, what she looked like, but my grandfather always said we were practically twins.

Forgetting that I was supposed to be going through all this stuff, I dropped to my knees next to the trunk. The picture wasn't posed, like in a studio, but was a candid shot. It was a little out of focus, and the top of my mother's head was cut off by the frame, but the photographer—whoever he or she was—had caught her in a moment of absolute joy.

I put the other pictures back into the trunk, but I slipped the one of my mother into the back pocket of my jeans. Looking inside again, I saw other items: a tiny jacket knit from rose-colored wool. A high-school graduation program. A wooden box that held a small golden crucifix. A handful of letters that started, "My dearest Margaret," written in my grandfather's neat penmanship.

This trunk must have been my grandmother's, and she had put things in here that were especially precious to her. I moved several other items aside and saw that at the very bottom of the trunk was an oddly shaped package, wrapped in heavy burlap and tied with twine.

It was about the size of a large book, maybe an encyclopedia, but it wasn't rectangular, like a box. It looked more like a triangle with one side carved away in an arc. I lifted the package out of the trunk carefully, trying not to sneeze from the dust cloud I raised.

I grasped the dry twine in my fingers, only to watch it crumble into fragments. Unwrapping the burlap, I saw a case inside. It was covered in some sort of leather. Curious, I pulled it free of the old cloth.

The leather was dark with age in spots, and mottled with stains that looked like water damage, but retained the color of coffee with cream and was as smooth and soft as the skin of my arm.

A shiver ran down the back of my neck. Something about the feel of it made me uncomfortable. I dropped it, wiping my hands on my jeans. What *was* it? I reached for it with an outstretched hand, almost having to force myself to touch it again.

There were marks of some kind scored faintly into the surface, but they were unlike any alphabet I'd ever seen. I'd studied ancient languages in my Literary Roots of Culture class during my freshmen year. They were not Roman, Sanskrit, Asian, or even hieroglyphics. The box had a small golden lock on it, and there was no key that I could see, in the wrapping or the trunk.

I prodded it gently with my finger and the lock sprang open with a soft click.

I opened the case and looked inside.

There was a wooden board cut in the same shape, with odd symbols burned into the surface. The signs looked like little pictographs, but were different than those on the leather case. I traced them with my finger: three wavy lines, one on top of the other. Water? Or maybe waves? A circle with lines radiating outward. That must be a sun. A skull and a crescent moon. What looked like a bird in flight. An outstretched hand, the fingers splayed open. I felt another odd chill on my skin when I placed my fingers on that shape. A horned goat, fainter than the others, and several other symbols that made no sense to me at all.

In one corner of the box was also a small triangular device that I recognized. It was a planchette, made out of what looked like ivory, with a long, thin pointer that came to a sharpened tip. It had been a long time since I'd seen one, at Jessica Tate's slumber party when I was a ten. But that cheap plastic board had looked nothing at all like this one.

I picked it up carefully, expecting it to be fragile, but the board felt solid in my hands, though ice cold, almost frozen, like a tree in winter. I settled it on my lap and let my fingers explore the surface of the wood. It was smooth beneath my skin, polished by hundreds, maybe thousands of hands touching it over the years. There were dark scorch marks on it here and there, as though the wood had once been in a fire. Tracing the outline of one of the symbols, I could feel the shallow cuts, their edges softened and rounded by the passage of time.

What is this thing? I wondered. And why had it been hidden at the bottom of my grandmother's trunk? My grandmother went to Mass every Sunday of her life. What on earth was she doing with a board that looked like some kind of weird occult artifact?

Did my grandmother actually believe in this kind of stuff? I wondered. I shook my head. I couldn't believe it. No matter how hard Kristen had tried to convince me, I personally didn't think things like séances, astrology, or fortune-telling were anything but scams used to take people's money. I was pretty sure that my grandmother felt the same way.

I couldn't help wondering, though, if the board still worked.

I picked up the planchette and placed it on the center of the board, then lightly rested my index and middle fingertips on either side of it. I imagined that it quivered beneath my fingers, just a little, and that I felt a surge of . . . something . . . rush through my body. I jumped, then laughed at myself. I must have imagined it.

A strange hum sounded in my ears, like a thousand voices all whispering at once.

"Grandpa?" I whispered. I closed my eyes. "Grandma?"

Nothing happened.

"Mom? Can you hear me?"

Still nothing.

Anybody? I whispered in my mind. *Is there anybody out there at all?*

Without warning, the planchette jumped in my hands and a cold breeze swept through the attic. I dropped the board.

"Nerves," I said to myself, thinking that there must be a crack in one of the windows. The breeze stirred again and I felt a sliver of ice slide down my spine.

Exhaling, I realized that I could see my breath in the air, and that I was also shivering. It had gotten colder in the attic and the planchette leaped again under my fingers, this time sliding smoothly across the surface of the board. The pointer stopped at the symbol that looked like a bird in flight—two lines like outstretched wings, and a long, smooth curve beneath them. Then it reversed course and stopped at the outstretched hand, then skidded over to the skull.

That's when I heard the voice whisper in my ear.

"Shalizander."

Snatching my fingers off the planchette, I jerked my head around. "Who's there?" I cried, but the attic was empty and dark. There was nothing, no one.

I was furious for allowing my imagination to run away with me. I had felt nothing more than a cold breeze in an old attic and a strange, useless board. I stared at the planchette, half-expecting it to move again on its own, but the notion was both silly and childish. Unrealistic.

I wanted to slam the board back into the case and hurl it across the room. Still, the board *was* beautiful and I couldn't bring myself to treat it badly. I started to put it carefully back into the case when a sudden noise from the first floor snared my attention.

I thought I heard a door crash open, and I paused, wondering if the wind had done it. I walked over to the stairs, listening. Just as I was about to consign the noise to the weather, I heard footsteps below. Someone was coming up the first flight of stairs.

I pulled back, wondering who it could be. I looked around for a handy weapon—a baseball bat or a hockey stick perhaps, but didn't see anything more suitable than an old coat rack.

Hiding wouldn't do any good. Not when the attic stairs

would have to be pulled back up and I could be stuck up here waiting for help for hours . . . and my cell phone was downstairs on the kitchen table. My choices were limited, and I didn't *want* to be afraid at this moment. Someone had broken in my grandfather's house.

My house!

"My Lord, there is a small problem."

"I am aware—the heir has woken the first Board."

"What are your wishes, my Lord?"

"For now, just watch her. Mark all who visit her and find out everything you can about them. We will not be the only ones interested in young Jenna Solitaire."

I tiptoed down the attic stairs, only half-aware that I still clutched the board in my hands. At the bottom of the steps, I saw him—the stranger from the funeral.

He looked up at me and his eyes went round and wide in surprise . . . or was it fear?

Suddenly, I was furious, a red mist of rage in front of my eyes. How dare this man . . . this stranger—come in to my home? How did he find out where I lived?

"Who are you? What do you want?" I yelled.

"Miss Solitaire, I need to tell you—" he started to say, his words tumbling over each other as he backed down the steps.

"It was you! You're the one who called yesterday and was taking my picture at my grandfather's funeral!" I held up the board in both hands, ready to heave it at him. "Get out!"

From the attic above me, a sudden, icy blast of wind swirled down the stairs. I saw the man's black cashmere coat flap around him like a living thing and he stumbled back a step or two. Several pictures hung in the hallway tilted crazily back and forth before falling to the floor and shattering.

Suddenly, the man turned and fled back the way he'd come. For a moment, I thought he was going to fall down the steps, but somehow he made it, stumbling and sliding on the carpet before regaining his balance and picking up speed again.

With the wind roaring in my ears, I found myself chasing him down the steps and into the living room. Dimly, I heard the doorbell ring and it crossed my mind that whoever was on the front step would stop the intruder. He slammed into the door, backed up, and threw it open. I heard a surprised grunt and then the thud of a body hitting the ground.

When I got outside, the stranger lay sprawled on the lawn, but one glance at me and he leaped to his feet again, running as if the demons of Hell itself were at his heels. I must have looked pretty angry, because I couldn't think of any other reason why a grown man who was willing to break into someone's house would run away from someone like me.

That's when I saw who had been ringing the doorbell. Father Andrew—and another man I didn't know. Father Andrew grabbed me by the shoulders as I tried to dart past him. "Jenna, what's going on?"

Gasping and trying to catch my breath, I pointed at the fleeing man. "He's the one who . . . took my picture . . . at the funeral. He broke into my house!"

The man standing next to Father Andrew immediately grasped the situation, turned, and sprinted after the intruder.

In Father Andrew's arms, I felt the winds that had been howling around me suddenly drop to a normal breeze. All my anger fled. I was suddenly aware of how afraid I'd been . . . and, at the same time, how powerful my anger had made me feel.

I watched the man race down the street, and relaxed in Father Andrew's arms. We didn't speak until a few minutes later when the man returned at a steady jog.

"I'm sorry," the man said, not even winded. "I lost him a couple of blocks from here." He shook his head. "Not as fast as I used to be."

"That's okay," I said. "What would you have done if you'd caught him?"

"Good point," he admitted with a strange smile, as if he knew exactly what he would do, and wasn't going to say. He looked at the board in my arms, but other than raising an eyebrow, didn't offer any comment.

Father Andrew herded us toward the door. "Let's get out of the cold," he said. "That breeze has a nasty bite."

I led the two men inside and closed the door. They followed me into the living room where Father Andrew offered up belated introductions. "Jenna Solitaire, this is Simon Monk; Simon, Jenna Solitaire."

"I'm pleased to meet you," the man said. He offered his hand. He was tall, with black hair and high cheekbones. Well-built and attractive, maybe in his early to mid-twenties, with a slight accent that probably drove women wild.

"Good to meet you, too," I said, shaking his hand. His eyes were a dark blue. Almost electric, like a flash of lightning in the night sky. Those piercing eyes met mine and I felt a flash of . . . something—and all the hairs on the back of my neck stood up. His grip was firm, and his hand large enough to completely swallow mine.

"Simon works for the Vatican," Father Andrew was saying. "And he happened to come by the church today."

"Yes, a stroke of luck," Simon said. "I'm doing genealogical research on the history of your family, Jenna. The Solitaire line is very old and quite interesting."

Perplexed, I said, "Really?"

"It's virtually a straight line," he said, sitting down and leaning back comfortably. "Female descendents only, who all kept their maiden name, going back many hundreds of years."

"*Hundreds* of years?" I asked. "My grandmother once told me that our name was an old tradition going back a long time, but I had no idea it was *that* long."

"Tell Jenna why the Vatican is interested in her heritage," Father Andrew said.

Simon nodded. "As you know, Father, the Vatican has a strong interest in genealogy. Family lines like yours that have belonged to the Church for so many years are of particular interest these days as . . . the number of our parishioners declines. It is hoped that by interviewing such families, we can gain insight into their faith and what has kept them such dedicated members of the Church for so long. In turn, the Vatican hopes to use this information to gain new converts."

I glanced at Father Andrew. Did *he* believe Simon's explanation? Because I sure didn't. I turned to Simon. "So you're a priest, then?"

Simon's face darkened. "No," he said. "I was once, but no longer."

"Once?" I asked.

"I do not discuss it," he said sharply.

There was something about his tone that nagged at me, almost as if his way of expressing annoyance was familiar, but I couldn't place it. We stared at each other for a long second and something in his eyes almost dared me to press him further, but I shrugged. I knew what it was like to not want to discuss some things.

"Okay," I said. "No big deal."

Father Andrew interrupted. "Jenna, it might be a good idea if you called the police."

"The police?" I asked. "Why?"

"The intruder you just chased out of your house," he reminded me.

I felt a strange jolt of surprise. I had been so wrapped up in talking with Simon that I'd completely dismissed the incident! Shaking my head, I excused myself to go make the call.

I brewed a pot of coffee while I answered the deputy's questions—no, the intruder didn't take anything . . . no, he didn't threaten me exactly . . . no, he wasn't still in the house . . . no, I heard myself agreeing, there wasn't much they could do.

Very helpful, I thought. *It's no wonder so many crimes go unreported.* I hung up the phone and poured three mugs of coffee. Setting them on a tray with containers of cream and sugar, I carried it back into the living room where Father Andrew and Simon were talking quietly.

"What did they say?" Father Andrew asked as I set the tray down on the table.

"Very little," I said. "There's nothing they can do."

Simon smiled grimly. "That's the police for you. It is much the same in Italy; they help when it is convenient."

I handed him a mug of coffee. He took it from me, sipped, and then pronounced it good. It was then I noticed the odd-looking coin on a necklace he wore.

A wave of dizziness swept over me, followed by an overwhelming feeling that I'd seen the necklace before. "Oh, how beautiful," I said, reaching for it. "May I take a closer look?"

His hand went to it immediately. "It is a coin from ancient Babylon. I have had it since I was a child."

Father Andrew chuckled. "Had it since you were a baby, you mean," he said. "Don't let him fool you, Jenna. He'd rather die a thousand deaths than let anyone touch it."

Simon shifted uncomfortably. "Perhaps we can continue our discussion?"

"Jenna makes the best coffee in town," Father Andrew said, sipping his with satisfaction. "It's why I stop over so much."

Smiling at him, I nodded. "Well, it isn't my baking," I said.

He laughed, his face reddening slightly. He'd once managed to choke down a slice of coffee cake I'd baked into submission with the help of three cups of coffee—but barely.

"No," he admitted. "It isn't."

We both laughed, and after a moment, Simon joined in. I sat down next to him on the couch.

"So, what is it you wanted to know exactly?" I asked.

"Oh, I'm mostly curious about any church-related activities of your family," Simon said. "You know, were they active participants in the church community? Altar boys when they were younger. That sort of thing."

"Interesting," I said, watching the way he tapped his fingers in sequence on the arm of the sofa. He seemed nervous. In fact, Simon's whole speech had the feel of something . . . preplanned or prepared, like he knew he'd need a story and had this one ready. I wondered what was going on behind his eyes, and was about to say something when Father Andrew stood up from the couch.

"Jenna, I'm sorry," he said, glancing at his watch. "I promised to meet with a parishioner today, and I've lost track of the time. I need to go."

"That's fine, Father," I said. "Thank you for coming by to check on me—and for introducing us." I turned to look at Simon. He wasn't a very accomplished liar. "I'm sure Simon and I will have plenty to talk about."

"I hope so," Father Andrew said, shrugging into his coat. "Are you doing okay, Jenna? Need anything at all?"

"I'm fine, Father," I told him. "Thank you."

"You're most welcome, my dear. If you need me, you know you can call anytime, right?" He opened the door, then paused and said, "By the way, Jenna, you know it wouldn't be a bad thing if I saw you at Mass on Sunday. It's been awhile."

I nodded. "I'll see what I can do, Father. I've been very busy with my studies, but I'll try my best."

He smiled at me, then stepped out and closed the door behind him. He was right, of course. It had been a long time since I'd attended Mass. I'd gone every Sunday as a child, but in high school my attendance slowly dwindled, and by the time I'd started college, I rarely went at all. I turned around to go back into the living room, and found Simon standing behind me.

Startled, I jumped backward with a little gasp, slipping on

the area rug in front of the door. Simon reached out and caught my arms, keeping me from falling.

"I didn't mean to startle you," he said.

"It's all right," I said, a little breathless. Caught off guard, I wondered why I felt so uncomfortable around him, why his touch caused goosebumps—and not the good kind—to break out on my arms. I shook my head and stepped out of his grasp.

"Thanks," I added. A quick mental vision of lounging in Simon's arms appeared in my head and I banished it immediately. I was *not* attracted to him, despite his good looks and cute accent.

"You're welcome," he said with a penetrating look that made me wonder if he could read my mind.

Blushing, I stammered, "So . . . shall we . . . finish our conversation?"

"Yes," he said. "Of course. I had only hoped to give Father Andrew my thanks and tell him I would stop by the church again later to see him."

"He was in a hurry," I said. "He tends to do that sometimes."

"Get in a hurry?" Simon asked, as we walked back to the living room.

"No," I said. "Forget something and then run off."

Simon gazed at me. "Do you know very much about your family history?" he asked. "For example, the earliest reference to a Solitaire female I can find goes back to France, around the mid-thirteen hundreds."

"You're kidding," I said. "That long ago?"

"Beyond a doubt," he said. "You come from an *enchanting* family line, Jenna."

His stress on the word "enchanting" was very odd, but I didn't understand what he meant by it, so I said, "Well, my grandfather always said my mother was enchanting as a young lady, if that's what you mean."

"I'm sure she was," Simon said. "But that's not quite what I meant."

A bit exasperated, I said, "So what *did* you mean?"

"We'll get to that," he said. "In due time."

I ground my teeth. I didn't appreciate Simon's cryptic little comments and was going to tell him that, but stopped myself. After all, he was a friend of Father Andrew's.

We sat back down in the living room and sipped our coffee for a moment. Outside, the wind started to swirl once more and I heard the patter-ping of stray raindrops on the window. After a short silence, Simon cleared his throat and I turned my attention back to him.

"Are you getting ready to tell me the real reason you're here?" I asked.

Simon smiled. "I didn't expect that you would believe my story, though it was good enough for Father Andrew."

"He's more trusting than I am," I said. "What *do* you want?"

"I'd like you to tell me about your mother, Moira."

"Why?" I asked. "I figured you'd want to talk about my grandfather, Michael, or even my grandmother, Margaret. They were the church-goers."

"I thought we'd already established that I wasn't here to

talk about the Church," Simon said. "My purpose is a bit more obscure than that."

"So I gathered," I said, "but before I start answering your questions, I'd like to know what your 'obscure' purpose is."

He smiled. "I'm researching some . . . interesting stories connected to your family," he said. "I cannot say more until I know more." Once again, his hand touched the coin necklace. It obviously had great significance for him.

I still didn't believe him, but it sounded like we were getting closer to the truth, and despite my discomfort around him, I didn't sense any real threat. "That will do for now," I said. "What do you want to know about my mother?"

"Anything you can remember," he said quickly. "Anything at all, but especially anything she might have told you about your family history."

"Sorry to disappoint you," I said, "but I don't really remember her very well. Some flashes of memory. Her face. Sometimes, I think, her voice."

"So she is dead then," he said.

It seemed like a strange way of putting it, as though he were seeking confirmation of the fact. "Yes," I said. "She died right after my fifth birthday."

"And your father?"

"In the same accident," I said. "A car crash." I could still remember being woken in the middle of the night, frightened at all the noise and upset, by my grandmother. She had held me for a long time, then carried me downstairs and told me both my parents were dead.

"I see," Simon said. "So then you were raised by your grandparents?"

"My grandfather mostly," I said. "My grandmother died a few years after my parents did."

"A difficult situation," he said. "I imagine raising a young girl was quite a challenge for him."

I smiled, memories flooding in. Strange, somehow he didn't seem so far away now, and I didn't feel so alone anymore. "He did just fine," I said. "He was a good man."

"I'm sure he was," Simon said. "Did your mother go to church regularly?"

"I really couldn't say," I said. "My grandfather told me she did when she was younger. Everyone in my family was raised in the Church, but then you know that or you wouldn't be here."

"Yes, yes, of course. What else do you remember about your mother? Do you recall any special personality traits?"

"She had red hair, like mine, and . . ." I let my words trail off. "What *is* your fascination with my mother? You keep pounding away on it, like you're expecting me to say something specific."

"Nothing in particular," he said quickly. His tone was defensive.

"Right," I said. "I've told you she died when I was a young child and that I have few memories of her, yet you keep asking questions about her. Care to try again?"

Simon sighed. "I knew you'd be too observant for this cha-

KEEPER OF THE WINDS

rade to go on much longer," he said softly. "From everything I've been told, the Solitaire women have all been the same."

"Everything you've been told?" I asked. "I don't understand."

"No, I suppose you wouldn't," he said.

"So, will you please tell me what you're *really* doing here and what it is you want to know?"

Simon leaned forward, staring at me intently. "I'm here to talk to you about the Board of the Winds, sometimes called the Board of Air."

Confused, I said, "The Board of what?"

"The Board of the Winds," he said. "You were carrying it in your arms when you chased the intruder out of your house." He paused, then added. "What do you know about it?"

"I . . . nothing," I said, thinking of the whispered word in the attic and the cold chill in the air. "I just found it in the attic."

"Surely your mother—or your grandmother—must have talked to you about it, left you a note?"

"No," I said. "It's just an old wooden board. It was in my grandmother's keepsake trunk." I looked at the board, which I'd set on the end table next to the couch. "Is that what this is all about? Some old board?"

"Jenna," Simon said. "The Board of the Winds is—you don't know anything about it, do you?" he asked. "I can hardly credit it."

"Credit *what?*" I said, trying not to yell. "I don't even know what you're talking about, and I don't even know who you really are." I picked up the board and clutched it to my chest. "If you're here to try and buy it, it's *not* for sale." I wondered why I suddenly felt so protective of it.

Simon held up his hands in surrender. "I have no intention of trying to buy it, Jenna. Nor do I wish to steal it from you, though there will be many people you encounter who would consider both—or worse."

Exasperated, I clenched my teeth and carefully sounded out each word. "*What . . . are . . . you . . . talking . . . about . . . ?*"

"The Board of the Winds," Simon said, "is an ancient magical artifact dating back to before the time of Christ." He looked at it appraisingly. "It is also your inheritance."

I shook my head. "The Board of the Winds is my inheritance? Like I told you, I found the board in my grandmother's keepsake trunk. Wouldn't an inheritance come in the form of a check or a letter or a package or something?" I realized I was starting to shout and tried to calm myself.

"What," I repeated, "in the world are you talking about?"

Simon stood up and said, "I'll be right back." Then he turned and went quickly up the stairs. Amazed, I listened as he made his way all the up to the attic, then returned several moments later with the case I'd found the board in. He set it down on the table. "Touch it," he said.

"I'd rather not," I admitted.

"Please," he said.

"Fine," I snapped, picking up the case. Once again, that

strange feeling of . . . wrongness crawled over my body. "The leather on this is . . . strange," I said.

"That is because it is made from human skin," Simon said.

"What?" I yelled, dropping the case and the board onto the carpet. "Are you serious?"

"Yes," he said. He picked up the case and brought it up to eye level. "If you look closely, you can still see the pores where the hair was removed before the skin was tanned."

Rubbing my hands on my jeans, I sat back down. "Why would my grandmother have an ancient Board of the—whatever you said—in a case made of human skin, for goodness sake? She was a good Catholic woman!"

"Winds," Simon said. "And I'm sure she was." He set the case down. "But she was also a Keeper. Just like your mother." He pointed at the board that sat on the living room floor. "For generations, the Solitaire women—one daughter only, born to each generation—has protected and carried that Board."

"I don't understand," I said. "Why?"

"Because it was their destiny—just as it is yours."

"My destiny?"

"The Board of the Winds, and the other Boards, are quite powerful and very evil. For some reason, only the Keeper can resist them." He pointed a long finger at me. "You are the Keeper of the Boards now."

"Me?" I asked. "And how can it be evil? It's an inanimate object!"

"According to my research, the Board is very much an entity unto itself. It's almost alive, in a way." His eyes locked onto mine. "I didn't expect to have to educate you about the Board. Traditionally, the Board has been passed down with instructions. Why don't I believe your innocent act? What are you up to?"

Outside the wind suddenly rose to a shriek, before quieting back down again. Simon looked pointedly at the Board and I felt my patience reach a breaking point. The charade had gone on far too long. A moment of silence stretched between us and, once again, I felt that strange connection to him. I didn't like it one bit.

"Now *I'm* the one who is making things up?" I said. "I just found it in the attic. I don't have any idea what you are talking about, and I have had *enough*."

"Jenna—"

"Out," I said, standing and pointing at the front door. "Right now. Take your . . . fantasy stories with you and go."

Simon stood up and began backing toward the door, when he suddenly stopped. "Jenna," he said, his tone deadly serious. "You didn't . . . you didn't attempt to *use* the Board when you found it, did you?"

Before I could answer, the wind howled again outside, and I heard the crack of a tree limb snapping and falling to the cold, frozen ground of early spring.

"She is visiting with a member of the clergy and a representative from the Vatican right now."

"Which one?"

"Simon Monk."

"Really? It seems the Knights have decided to get involved as well. All of them are so predictable it's pathetic. Neither the Vatican nor the Knights have any idea what they are fooling with here. Which will work in our favor. Remain vigilant. And spread the word to your other contacts in town. There will be a handsome reward for whoever brings me the Board."

"Okay, *that's* it," I said. "Get out."

"Jenna, hold on a minute—" Simon started to say.

"No, no holding on a minute, a second, or anything. My life is difficult enough, thanks, without ex-priests visiting me the day after my grandfather's funeral and trying to scare me. It wouldn't surprise me if you were somehow working with that guy who broke into my house!" I pointed at the door. "Out."

Simon shook his head. "Jenna, I really think we should talk more."

"And I really think you should get your butt out the door more," I snapped. "It's been a long day, and I've already called the police once."

"There are things about the Board you need to know, Jenna," Simon said, walking backward as I shoved him toward the door. "It's not a toy!"

"I'm sure it isn't," I said. "I know, I heard you—it's a magical artifact from ancient times made to do who knows what." I took his overcoat off the hook by the door and threw it at him. "Out!"

"Jenna, you need to know the truth!" he protested. "Let me help you, please."

"Oh, give me a break!" I yelled. I threw open the door and shoved him outside into the wind and the rain. "Enough already."

Simon started to speak again, something about how I needed to listen to him, and I slammed the door shut in his face, and threw the deadbolt. "Jeez!" I said. "Every town has one and ours just got a new one."

Stomping into the kitchen, I wondered if Father Andrew knew that his visitor from the Vatican was, in fact, some kind of a kook. Sure, he was cute, but if the man believed my grandmother was holding onto an ancient magical artifact stored in a case made of tanned human skin, then I was the tooth fairy. I set the cups into the sink, vowing to wash them later.

"What a day," I muttered, wondering what I'd done to deserve the sudden influx of weirdness in my life. Looking at the clock on the wall, I saw that it was almost three. I'd been hoping to get more done, but I was completely wrung out. I picked up the phone and called Tom.

He answered on the third ring. "Jenna! How are you?"

I hated it when he did that—used caller ID instead of just saying hello—but I resolved to not let it bother me. "Hey, Tom," I said. "I'm good, how are you?"

There was a long pause, then, "I know you hate it when I do that," he said.

I waited.

"Don't you?" he asked.

I sighed. "Yes, Tom, you *know* I hate it when you do that."

"Then why didn't you *say* so?"

"I just did," I snapped. "Happy now?"

"Ouch," he said. "Long day at the office?"

He was right. I was cranky and it showed. "Something like that," I admitted. "It's been a long few days."

"I know it has," he said, his voice contrite. "Just trying to cheer you up, I guess."

"It's okay," I said. "I could use the cheering."

"How are you holding up?"

"Other than the weird board I found in the attic, an intruder in the house, and a bizarre visit from a man who claims to work for the Vatican, life is good," I said.

"What?" Tom asked. "What's going on?"

I told him about finding the board, the man breaking in, and my visit from Father Andrew and Simon Monk. *What kind of a name is Simon Monk anyway?* I wondered. I didn't tell Tom about the whispered word I'd heard—or *thought* I'd heard—in the attic.

"Wow," he said when I finished filling him in. "You've stepped into the Twilight Zone, Jenna."

"You're telling me," I said. "I just want out."

I heard the clack of computer keys in the background and then the music from the show started. Rod Serling did his voice-over and Tom chanted along.

I did smile then, and even managed a laugh. "You've always been good at cheering me up, Tom," I said. "Look, it's been a long day. Do you want to hook up tomorrow for lunch or something?"

"Sure," he said. "Meet me at the Cramp-us Café?"

The Cramp-us Café was actually the College Café in the student union, but ever since a well-publicized food poisoning incident early in the semester, people had been calling it the *Cramp-us*. Given the quality of the food, the name was a perfect fit.

"Why not?" I said. "I've got to be on campus anyway—I'm behind on my work—and I've got to eat something, even if it may kill me."

"Good deal," he said. "I'll meet you around eleven-thirty or so. Kristen's class ends around one, so she'll join us later, okay?"

"Great," I said. "Have a good night, Tom, and . . . thanks. Thanks for making me smile."

"You're welcome, Jenna. See you tomorrow," he said, then hung up.

I looked around the kitchen and shrugged. The dishes could wait. The attic could wait. All I wanted to do was go to sleep. I felt like I'd been swimming in mud all day, and I was exhausted. Maybe a shower and a decent night's rest would make the world seem a little less like a comic book and a little more like the life I'd known before my grandfather had died.

. . . Shalizander . . . you can hear us, can't you? Our voices are loud in your ears. Our hungers are your hungers.

"No!"

You can use us. You can control us. The others were weak. You are strong. Open the way.

"Never! I won't!" *I feel the sweat pouring out of my skin. The room is hot, filled with liquid flames—like I'm standing in a bonfire.*

Shalizander, you dream the power dreams. It was your vision, too.

"Not anymore," *I say.* "You will not be used."

If not you, then someone else. Someone weaker. Someone whose blood doesn't sing like yours. The hunger for power is absolute. You hunger, too.

Screaming, I shove the Boards off the worktable. "Never!"

47

"Never!" I screamed, sitting up in bed, scattered fragments of the dream clinging to me like a spider's web.

Next to me, the phone jangled a shrill ring. Half-awake, I answered it. "Hello?"

"Have you started hearing the voices yet?" The voice was male and familiar.

"What?" I asked. "Voices?"

"The voices," the caller said. "The voices of the Boards."

My brain caught up to my body. "Simon Monk, right?" I asked. An image of him rose in my mind, the strength of his hands and face, the intensity of his eyes . . . even the way he touched that coin necklace.

"Yes," he said. "Jenna, the Board is—"

I hung up the phone. Just what I needed. A *persistent* weirdo. Shaking my head, I climbed out of bed and went to the window. Off and on all night, the spatter of wind-driven rain had pelted my window, pulling me from sleep. Today's weather looked to offer more of the same—gray, wind, rain, cold.

My eyes felt like sandpaper. *So much,* I thought, *for a good night's rest.*

And as always, my dreams had the disturbing force of reality. I lived more in my sleep than most people did during their waking hours. It was exhausting. I looked at my bedside clock and started—it was almost ten in the morning! I'd been dreaming for hours, and I never slept that long. I thought back over what I could remember of the night and realized that while I could recall the last dream I'd had—a very strange series of images and odd, sibilant voices and a stack of boards that looked similar to the one I'd found in my attic—all the other dreams I'd ever remembered having were gone. Only black spaces remained in my memory.

Shalizander . . .

I wondered who or what Shalizander was, and I found myself staring at the dresser where I'd set the board, put away in its case, before going to bed. Was Simon Monk a freak, or did the Board really represent something ancient and evil?

I didn't know, that was certain, but I felt sure I knew someone who did. Jonathan Martin—one of my professors at school who taught several courses in ancient cultures, arts, and iconography. If anyone would know what the Board was, or at least what some of the strange symbols on it meant, it would be him. I thought he had office hours today, so perhaps I could arrange to see him after I met Tom for lunch.

Happy to have a course of action at last, I quickly dressed, gathered up my books and the Board, and headed for the campus.

"What do you make of this?" I asked, taking the board case out of my backpack and showing it to Tom.

He took the case from me, his left eyebrow unconsciously rising in curiosity.

"What is that?" he asked. "Some kind of leather?"

"Something like that," I said, thinking of Simon telling me it was human skin and unable to repress a shudder. I didn't know why, but for some reason I believed him. It probably wasn't a good idea to mention *that* particular fact to Tom right now.

"It feels . . ." Tom said, his words drifting off as he looked for the right adjective and failed to come up with it. "I don't know."

"Me, either," I admitted. "So, what do you think?"

Without answering, Tom shook his head and slowly opened the case. When he saw the Board, he whistled softly. "I can't say I've ever seen anything quite like it."

"I know," I said. "Look at the symbols. They aren't Sanskrit or even Egyptian."

Tom nodded. "I don't recognize them either." He closed the case. "Maybe we should do some digging in the library and online, see if we can find out anything useful."

I looked at my watch. Professor Martin's office hours started at two. I still had plenty of time. "Sure, but you can do the online looking—you know I prefer good old-fashioned books to computers. There's something about a book that just feels better to me than a computer."

Tom grinned. "You use them to send and receive e-mail all the time."

I sighed. "Tom, your grandmother sends and receives

e-mail. Everyone does e-mail. It's the other things I'm terrible at."

"I know," he said, "but I won't hold it against you."

"Come on," I said, and pulled him in the direction of the campus library, feeling better than I had in days.

"Jenna, take a look at this," Tom said, gesturing at the computer screen.

I put down the book on ancient symbols I'd been paging through and stood up to peer over Tom's shoulder. On the screen was a series of images almost exactly like the ones on the Board. A chill went up my spine. "Where did you find those?"

"I used that goat's head symbol as a starting point, and it led me here," he said, clicking the mouse on the BACK button. Another page loaded, this one with huge lettering at the top reading THE TEMPLAR KNIGHTS: A MAGICAL HISTORY.

"According to this site, the Templar Knights were accused of all kinds of magical things." He pointed to a specific section of the text. "Apparently, the symbols I just showed you were found in some of their texts and used as proof of their demon worship."

"Demon worship?" a voice said behind us, the sound echoing in the quiet library.

Tom and I both jumped and turned around. Kristen was standing behind us. Today she was wearing a dark purple velvet dress, and several studded bracelets with a matching necklace. I tried not to stare.

"Since when are you two interested in demon worship?" she asked. "I had no idea."

"Kristen," Tom said, trying to stop her before she could start. "We're *not* interested in demon worship."

"Of course you aren't," she said. "Demon worship involves all kinds of nastiness, sacrificing animals or people, dancing naked while drinking blood from a skull cup under a full moon—or is that a druidic thing?—anyway," she continued, and I wondered how she managed to breathe while speaking that much, "believe me, you don't want to go worshipping any demons." Even when she said the most outlandish things, Kristen *sounded* so knowledgeable and serious that it was hard not to believe her.

Of course, if I wanted to retain my sense of reality at all, I had to take everything she said with a large dose of salt.

"We don't!" I said. "We were just doing some research for our Cults—Then and Now class."

"Oh, cool," she said, leaning on the side of Tom's chair. "How did I miss that in the catalog? A class on the occult?"

"You were probably distracted with . . . something else," Tom said, and I felt instantly grateful that he hadn't said anything about the Board. I couldn't say why, but for some reason, I knew I wanted the Board to be kept secret. I knew I could trust Tom with anything and everything, even something as strange as the Board.

"I can help, if you'd like," Kristen said. "I know all about the occult."

Tom and I laughed. "Kristen," I said. "That's because you study everything you might *want* to believe in."

"Not true!" she said. "I don't believe in . . ." her voice trailed off while she tried to come up with something.

"Werewolves?" Tom suggested.

"Vampires?" I added.

"No," she said, grinning. "Leprechauns. I don't believe in those."

Tom and I exchanged a glance and he said, "Kristen, I love you, you know that, but how can you believe in vampires and werewolves, but not leprechauns?"

She leaned down and kissed him. "Because they aren't at all *romantic*," she said. "It's easy to believe in romance."

Tom smiled and shook his head.

"Drinking blood is romantic?" I asked. "To each his own, I suppose."

"No," Kristen said. "For vampires, drinking blood is necessary. Eternal love is romantic."

I shrugged. For me, love and romance weren't part of my daily life—at least they hadn't been lately. I had dated some, but had never been able to sustain a serious relationship. I wasn't sure why, though my grandfather always said it was because my looks intimidated the boys. I didn't believe that for a minute, but maybe I just hadn't met the right man yet.

For some reason, this thought brought an image of Simon's face into my mind, and I quickly banished it. He was crazy, but the man had somehow gotten into my head, and getting rid of him was going to be harder than I expected.

"So, what are you trying to find out?" she asked.

"Just looking up some symbols right now," I said. "Getting ideas."

"Oh," Kristen said, looking crestfallen, then her face brightened. "Maybe you could do something on healing crystals."

"Healing crystals?" Tom asked.

"Yeah," she said. "Like the one I gave Jenna at the funeral. You've still got it on you, right?"

"Actually, I do," I said, pulling it out of my purse where I'd promptly put it and then forgotten it existed. I held it up for her to see.

"Good," she said. "You should carry it with you all the time."

Before I could say anything else, Tom interrupted me. "Aren't you supposed to be seeing Professor Martin?"

I glanced at my watch and realized that we'd been in the library for almost two hours. Where had the time gone? Professor Martin's office hours were almost over!

"I've got to run if I'm going to catch Professor Martin," I said. "Can we meet up later?"

"Sure," Tom said. "Did you find what you needed?"

"A few leads," I hedged, glancing at Kristen, "but nothing concrete."

"Well, we'll figure it out," he said. "I'll call you later."

"And I can help, too!" Kristen said. "Maybe Atlantis would be a good project. Or the cults at King Solomon's mines?"

"Maybe," I said, shouldering my backpack. "We'll talk later."

"Later," they said in unison.

As I jogged for the exit, I wondered how two people that were so different could sustain a relationship. Maybe there was something to the old cliché of opposites attracting.

I pushed against the door, and when it didn't open, slammed into it hard enough to knock my head against the glass. "What the . . ." I mumbled, then shoved against it again.

Straining, I managed to get it open a crack and heard the high, thin whistle of the wind coming in. Looking out, I saw that many of the smaller trees on campus were bent over and clusters of clouds were racing across the gray sky. The wind had grown into a full force gale and created a vacuum on the door seals.

I shoved harder, and finally managed to get it open.

The wind caught me in its grasp, and it was all I could do to hold onto the door and not fly back into the building. Struggling, I forced myself to the opposite side of the door and let the wind shut it behind me. It slammed hard enough to rattle the glass in the windows.

I pushed forward, leaning against the freakishly strong wind and started toward the building where Professor Martin's office was. It felt like I was walking in a wind tunnel . . . or reliving my dreams. Another shiver worked its way up my spine.

All around me, the air was filled with flying debris: dead

leaves, papers, bits of trash all swirled through the air, caught briefly on light poles or statues, and then blown off again. Weather this severe was very odd for Miller's Crossing, Ohio, but probably wouldn't have been out of place in Nebraska or Kansas. From what I had been told, the wind there blew like this most every day, though that might have been an exaggeration.

I ducked as a gigantic wet leaf went twirling by my head and forced myself to hurry.

I needed Professor Martin's advice about the Board, and no wind was going to keep me from getting there before he left.

"My Lord, she is at the local college now. This may be our best opportunity. Also, she rebuffed Simon."

"Did she? Our little pseudo-Keeper is stronger willed than I thought. Unless . . . yes, perhaps the Board has already begun speaking to her. Very interesting, indeed."

"One of our contacts claims he can get the Board—today."

"If he can, more power to him, then no one would even know that we were involved."

Every college had at least one professor, I suspected, like Professor Martin. Well-traveled, intelligent, and *very* eccentric. His small office was overloaded with books on innumerable subjects and strange knickknacks from odd corners of the world he had visited. On one shelf, *something* floated in a jar of thick, clear liquid, while on another a small doll shared space with a strangely formed animal skull. Going into Professor Martin's office was a little like visiting a zoo, a library, and an unorganized closet all at once.

I loved it. And I liked Professor Martin a lot. So far, all three classes I'd taken with him had been great. His door was open a crack and I knocked lightly on it.

"Come forth," Professor Martin called out.

"Hello, Professor," I said.

"Jenna!" he said. "What brings you here? I don't have you in any of my classes right now, do I?" For a moment, I could see him trying to remember every face in each course he taught and failing miserably. He was a tall man, and underweight, with thinning blond hair and a style of dress Tom and I'd dubbed "Broke College Professor" soon after we'd started taking his Introduction to Ancient Cultures class. Tom was a computer science major, and didn't think anthropology was even a proper science, but I'd managed to talk him into taking the course anyway.

I laughed. "No, not this semester," I said. "Though I'm planning on taking the Arts & Icons of South America next semester."

"Good," he said. "You'll add a lot to our discussions."

"Thanks," I said. "I'm looking forward to it. But I stopped by for another reason."

"Oh?" he said, his eyebrows raised with curiosity. "What's that?"

I pulled my backpack off my shoulder and removed the board case. "I was cleaning out my grandfather's attic, and I found this." I held out the case to him.

"Yes," he said. "I'm sorry for your loss."

The words were kind, but meaningless. His attention was

riveted on the case. He moved his hands over it with gentle care, rubbing the burned-in symbols, his eyes wide with wonder.

"This is amazing," he mumbled, then he opened the case.

His inhalation would have been audible in the hallway, even over the wind. "Fantastic!" he said. He removed the Board from its case and set it gently on the desk. "I've never seen anything quite like it."

"Oh," I said. "I was hoping you knew what it was."

He traced his fingers over the symbols on the Board. "I could make an educated guess," he said. "But I'd rather be certain before I said too much of anything." He pointed. "Some of these symbols are Babylonian, some of the others look more arcane than that."

He gazed at me through the smudged lenses of his glasses. "Was your grandfather ever in the Middle East?"

I shook my head. "No, I don't think so. And the Board belonged to my grandmother."

"Hmm . . ." he said. "It's quite a piece. Quite lovely . . . and the case! Do you know what it is?"

"I was told it was human skin," I said, trying to repress another shudder.

"That's exactly right," Professor Martin said, his voice getting louder. "Incredibly rare and often associated with the black arts. Such perfect examples are almost never seen in this day and age."

"It really *is* human skin?" I asked. "Who would do a thing like that?"

The professor shrugged. "I've read of ancient sorcerers who believed that human skin made the best leather, especially if it came from a willing sacrifice. In some cultures it was rumored that slaves could buy their freedom with the skin from their back. A horrid practice, to be sure, but fascinating."

"I'd just call it disgusting," I said. "Can you tell me anything else about it?"

Professor Martin shook his head. "Not off hand," he said. "There's something familiar about it, but I can't quite seem to recall . . ." His voice trailed off, then he snapped his fingers. "Jenna, would you mind if I kept it for a short while—a day or two perhaps? I have a colleague who might be able to shed some light on this."

My first thought was one of relief, that someone might know *something* about the Board . . . something that might explain why it was in my grandmother's belongings to begin with. But before I could open my mouth to agree I felt an almost painful lurch in my stomach, and I thought I heard that voice again. *"Shalizander."*

I looked around the room, wondering if Professor Martin had heard it as well, but he just stared at me expectantly.

The Board was mine, and I couldn't believe I'd even been considering letting him have it. "No," I said. "I'm sorry, but I don't feel comfortable with that."

His eyebrows arching, Professor Martin said, "I don't understand, Jenna. I thought you wanted my help."

"I do. I just . . . I don't know . . . I don't want . . . it's important that I keep the Board with me."

"Don't be silly," he said. "While it is certainly unique, I have no intention of keeping it from you. I merely wanted to show it to a colleague of mine in the hope that he might be able to offer more information." He gestured at the case. "There are many occult societies, Jenna, that treasure such artifacts as this. There is even one associated with the symbol on your medallion."

I remembered then that I was still wearing my grandmother's necklace. "This?" I asked, pulling it out from beneath my hair. "What do you mean?"

"The Templar Knights used that very symbol as the marking of one of their secret societies. A sub-group, in fact, concerned with the worship of demons and the creation and acquisition of magical devices and relics. They were supposedly wiped out shortly after the death of one of their Grandmasters—a man named Jacques de Molay."

For some reason, the name struck a chord within me. And Tom and I had seen that information online about the Templar Knights. Perhaps the man's name had been mentioned in the text. "So you think my grandmother was in a secret society of Templar Knights?"

"Not at all," Professor Martin said, laughing. "The symbol is very ornate and decorative. No doubt the jeweler who made the necklace had seen it somewhere, thought it pretty, and used it as a design without even knowing what it was."

"Then why mention the Templars?"

"My friend," he said, "is well-versed in such esoteric history. I hoped he might be able to give us a clue about the

Board, perhaps because it might have been mentioned in one of the many texts he has studied." He shrugged. "It was a suggestion."

Once again, I thought of giving him the Board—he seemed so earnest, but . . . something wasn't right. My grandfather had always told me that I had good instincts. I couldn't explain it, but what I was feeling from Professor Martin wasn't helpfulness, but longing. He *wanted* the Board for himself, and I didn't know why. The way he continued to stroke the edges of it with his hands, and how his gaze kept returning to it while we talked . . . it felt as though he wasn't really paying attention to me.

I shut the board case and stuffed it in my backpack. The sudden urge to flee from his office was overwhelming. "I'll think about it, Professor," I said. "I've got to go now."

He stood up, his smile fading and his cheeks turning an ugly shade of red. "Jenna, I can't help you if you act like this."

His voice was almost patronizing, like he expected me to obey.

"Fine, Professor," I snapped, just wanting to get away from him. "Then don't help. Sorry I asked. I've to go." I turned and almost ran out the door.

Behind me, I heard him yell, "Jenna! Come back!" But I kept running.

I crossed the parking lot, head down against the wind. A few other students crossed the campus as well, all of them struggling to either keep from being pushed forward or back by the gale. Voices and debris were torn away with equal ferocity, so I barely heard the sound of my name being called.

"Jenna! Jenna Solitaire!"

I turned around to see Simon Monk on the far side of the parking lot. Had he been following me? I made it to my car and managed to get the back door open enough to toss my pack in the backseat. He reached me just as I slammed the door shut and whirled around, my hair whipping across my face.

"Now what do you want?" I asked. "Can't you just leave me alone?"

"I'm trying to help you, Jenna," Simon said. "There are things you need to know."

"I'm sure there are," I said.

"Look, did you find the journal?"

"What journal?" I asked.

"According to my research, it's sometimes called the Chronicle of the Keepers. It's been around for as long as the Board, and it chronicles the history of the Board and those who have protected it."

I nodded while slowly reaching for the door handle. This man may have been a priest, and he may even have worked for the Vatican, but that didn't mean he wasn't crazy.

"A book that's as old as the Board? Nope, sorry, haven't seen it." I opened the door. "And now if you'll excuse me . . ."

"Jenna, please," Simon said, reaching out to touch my arm.

I found myself caught in his gaze once more and fought to look away.

"The Board isn't some toy you can just show off to your friends. It is a powerful artifact and many people would willingly kill for it."

Kill for it? I shivered, remembering the way Professor Martin's eyes kept shifting to the Board when we were talking. I held up my hand to forestall his next comment. "Listen, Simon, you seem like a pretty nice guy. A little crazy, but a nice guy. Now, I'm going to have to ask you to get out of the way and *leave me the hell alone*. Get it? Got it? Good." I got into my car and shut the door.

For once, the engine started on the first try. I half-expected Simon to start pounding on the window and demanding I listen to more of his ranting, but he simply stood there in the wind and watched me drive away.

Heading home, I decided to do two things. First, the next time I saw Father Andrew, I was going to give him a piece of my mind—priest or not—for introducing me to a man who was obviously some kind of stalker. Possibly a crazed stalker. Second, I was going to get back up in the attic and see if I couldn't find some more clues about the Board or why my grandmother had it in the first place.

Driving my little car through the wind and watching swollen banks of rain-laden clouds race overhead, I wondered if Simon might have been telling the truth. Was there a journal? For all that he was a borderline nutcase, he seemed to know a lot about the Board itself. Where would my grand-mother have kept it?

And Professor Martin's explanation of my grandmother's medallion seemed a little too pat to me. Why would some jeweler put a design on it and not know what it meant? Did my grandmother know someone in this secret Templar Knight society? It hardly seemed plausible, and yet there had to be some reason for all of this.

My hands knew the way home, so I let my mind drift into memory, seeking any clue or hint that my grandmother had been anything other than what she had appeared: a sweet old lady who loved going to church and gardening. Turning onto my street, I shook my head. Nothing. Nada. Not even a hint of impropriety or weirdness that I could remember. And wouldn't my grandfather have told me if he'd known? I thought so; it had been just the two of us for so long that keeping secrets from each other was difficult.

He'd known the first time I kissed a boy—Ricky Lynton from two blocks down the street—and the first time I'd fallen in love. He knew everything about me, and I knew everything about him; from how he loved to listen to baseball on the radio, but hated to watch it on television to his secret desire to write a spy novel set during the Korean conflict and his fascination with history. He *would* have told me something this . . . this extraordinary if he'd known about it. I was positive.

I pulled up to the house, grabbed my pack out of the backseat, and hurried inside. A brief lull in the wind made the walk less of a struggle. I unlocked the front door, stepped in, and closed it behind me. Listened to the silence and felt . . . safe. Yes, I had the Board with me and I was safe.

It was strange to realize that I'd become so attached to it. Perhaps it was the mystery of it all, of what my grandfather had or hadn't known, of what my grandmother might have been doing with it in the first place. I took off my jacket and hung it in the hall, then went into the kitchen to start some fresh coffee. There was nothing like a hot cup of gourmet coffee on a cold, windy, rainy day . . . and even though the chills I'd been feeling weren't all related to the weather, the warmth would be nice.

I left my backpack and the Board on the kitchen table, and took my coffee mug into the one room of the house I almost never entered: my grandfather's bedroom.

It was part of our living style that we did not enter the other person's room without permission. Unfortunately, he wasn't here to give me permission. I stood outside his door, which had been shut since the day he died, and worked my-self up to opening it. In fact, I hadn't been in this room in . . . at least a year. We had always believed that people needed a private space to call their own and tried to respect that as much as possible.

The house was quiet and empty. "Too much private space," I said aloud. I felt a little like a thief, sneaking into his room when he wasn't here to tell me not to. Yet, I had to know more about the Board, and going up to the attic again was an even less appealing prospect.

I reached out and opened the door to his room.

The shades were drawn and only a little light crept in from the two windows on the far side of the room. I flicked on the overhead switch. The bed was made up, a green quilt my grandmother had made years before folded and hung over the footboard. A masculine jewelry box sat on top of the antique dresser. A small reading lamp on the nightstand next to the bed was turned off, and next to it was the book my grandfather had been reading. The fading scent of his aftershave brought a sting to my eyes. He'd been wearing it for years, and I would probably always associate that warm, buttery smell with him and the safety of his arms.

Not really knowing where to start, I crossed the room and opened the shades. The gray light did little to cheer me, so I also turned on the reading lamp. Its warm yellow radiance drove back some of the shadows. I moved the book aside and saw that he had left his watch on the nightstand instead of putting it in the jewelry box on his dresser.

The nightstand had one drawer, and still feeling like a thief, I opened it. I consoled my conscience by reminding myself that I would have to go through his things eventually. The open space beneath the drawer was filled with books, and if my grandfather had hidden anything in his room, it would be in a drawer or his closet.

Inside, I saw that he had a bible and a stack of letters. I flipped through them, and found myself smiling. They were love letters from my grandmother. He had saved hers, just as she had saved his. I picked up the Bible, which I hadn't seen before, and a sealed envelope dropped out of it. In my grandfather's handwriting, I recognized my name. Excited and curious, I wondered why he had left it here for me to find, or if that was what he had intended at all.

I tore open the envelope and removed the single sheet of paper from within it, then started to read:

> *My Dearest Jenna,*
>
> *If you are reading this now, I must be dead. It is not in your nature to go through my things without permission, so I have no doubt that I am gone. I am so sorry for you, my dear. You have been left alone in the world, and for that I can only pray that you have the strength to carry on.*
>
> *I could not put this letter in my estate materials. The lawyer would have thought I was suffering from Alzheimer's. There is something you must know and little I can tell you . . . as close as I was to your grandmother and your mother, the secrets kept in a woman's heart are deep.*
>
> *In the attic, you will find a trunk with your grandmother's belongings, including a strange board that she told me was called the Board of the Winds. I overheard her and your mother once talking about it, and referring to themselves as its Keepers. What this all means, I do not know, but I do know one thing: you were meant to have the Board and protect it, just as your mother was. When she died, your grandmother took the Board out of your*

mother's house and brought it here along with you.

I wish I could tell you more, my precious Jenna, but there is little else I can say. I questioned your grandmother often about it, but she wouldn't speak of it, and she died before I could do more than ascertain that you were to play some role in the Board's fate and that she was keeping a journal of some kind for your reference.

I have never been able to find the journal, Jenna, but it must be here in Miller's Crossing. She spoke of it just a few days before she died. If you can find it, perhaps it will guide you where I could not.

Don't be scared, Jenna. I have always felt that some amazing destiny awaited you; your grandmother felt the same. Seek it out, my dear . . . you are too bright a star for this sleepy town. Go out into the world and shine.

Loving You Always,
Your Grandfather

I felt the hot sting of tears on my cheek and I wondered what a Keeper was and where the journal—that Simon obviously knew existed—could have been hidden. If it took me all night, I'd tear the house apart and find it.

I had to have answers about this mystery that had entered my life and turned it upside down.

I reached up and grasped the medallion that had belonged to my grandmother, peering at it closely. Secret societies and keepers and magical boards? None of it made sense, and yet I felt a stirring within me that I could not deny.

I pulled the necklace off and studied it again. Sitting on my grandfather's bed, the letter beside me, I wondered how long my grandmother had worn the medallion. I wasn't sure, but my grandfather had told me that she wore it every day.

The metal was smooth and warm from resting against my skin and I traced the odd design on the front. Strangely, the medallion's weight didn't match its thickness. It should be heavier, and I hadn't noticed it before. But there were no hinges that would have hinted that it was a locket.

I tapped lightly on it with my fingernail and listened carefully. Yes, it *was* hollow. Puzzled, I tried to figure out how to open it. There was no obvious latch and not even a visible seam, yet . . .

The design wrapped from the front to the back, in an obvious pattern. It ended in an odd, star-shaped symbol right in the center of the back. Guessing, I pressed down on it hard and heard a sharp click from within.

The two halves of the medallion fell open and a small slip of paper landed on the floor. Setting the pieces aside, I picked up the tiny piece of paper and unfolded it.

It read ST. ANNE'S. MOTHER MARY. 3ʳᵈ FROM RIGHT.

I stared at the small script in stunned disbelief. Could all of this somehow be true? Was Simon right about my grandmother—and my mother—being some kind of . . . special Keeper?

Could the Board truly be a magical artifact?

I didn't know for sure, but I intended to find out.

> *"My Lord, our contact failed. She still has the Board, and Simon accosted her again in the parking lot. We almost intervened—"*
>
> *"And it is well that you didn't. The more Simon rambles on about what he thinks he knows, the less likely it is that she will believe him."*
>
> *"She's going to the church where her grandfather was buried."*
>
> *"It's time to bring this to a close. Collect her—and the Board—there, but keep it quiet."*

I had told Father Andrew that I would think about coming to Mass on Sunday, but a visit to St. Anne's was necessary now. Plus, he still had a lot to answer for as far as Simon Monk went.

I hadn't been able to figure out how to put the medallion back together, so I'd slipped the paper in my pocket, grabbed my backpack, and headed for the church. The winds had dropped to mere spring whispers again, so at least I wasn't wandering in a hurricane like earlier that day.

Parked outside the church, I saw Father Andrew's car in his reserved spot. He was here somewhere, probably in his office, but the grounds were large enough that looking for him would take some time.

I wasn't sure what the note my grandmother had left meant, but St. Anne's had been a part of my grandparents' lives every week for years. Miller's Crossing was a small enough town that the church was still left open twenty-four hours a day, for those who wanted to come in and pray at odd hours.

Leaving the shelter of my car, I slung my backpack over my shoulders and crossed the parking lot. As I stepped inside, childhood memories flooded my mind. This is where I'd been baptized, learned my catechisms, and become an adult. Off the main sanctuary, there was a little chapel dedicated to the Virgin Mary, and I made the sign of the cross out of long habit before entering.

It was a reflexive gesture and it caught me off guard. I hadn't been to church in a long time, and while I still believed in God, my connection to Him was distant, like a childhood memory.

I sat down in a pew and whispered a prayer under my breath. "Mother Mary, I think . . . I don't know what to think, but if you can help me find what my grandmother wanted me to, I would be thankful."

For some reason, the prayer made me feel better.

On the altar, candle votives flickered in the subtle drafts of air in the church. A dim glow of light spread across the blue altar cloth and the painted image of Mary, gently looking down on her supplicants. That small, sad smile is on her lips, as though she feels sorry for the folly of her children.

I pulled the slip of paper out of my pocket and studied it again: ST. ANNE'S. MOTHER MARY. 3ʳᵈ FROM RIGHT. Well, this was St. Anne's and I was standing in front of Mother Mary. What was third from the right? I looked at the gilt frame and saw nothing that could be a hidden anything. Frustrated, I started poking at the embossed flowers on the frame, grumbling to myself.

"Jenna? What brings you here?" a voice said behind me.

My startled scream echoed through the whole church, and I spun around with my heart in my throat.

Father Andrew caught my arms. "Whoa," he said. "I'm sorry to have frightened you. Are you all right?"

"I'm . . . I'm fine, Father," I said. "I was just . . . how are you?" I sounded like an idiot to myself, so there was no doubt that he must have thought I'd lost my mind.

"I'm fine," he said. "Were you lighting a candle for your grandfather?"

I nodded. Now I was lying to a priest and in church. *Perfect.*

"I just stopped by for a minute," I said, hoping he would accept my lame excuse and not ask me why I'd been poking at the picture frame.

"I understand," he said. "How are you getting along?"

I suddenly remembered that I was going to talk to Father Andrew about Simon. "I meant to ask you. You do know that Simon Monk is not completely sane, don't you? He's obsessed."

"Why would you say that?" he asked. "Simon is a very learned man, Jenna. And highly respected in the Church."

"He thinks this board I found is some kind of magical artifact and he *lied* about why he wanted to meet me." I didn't mention, of course, that I'd just lied, too, but that was because it didn't seem relevant at the time.

"Well, lying *is* wrong," Father Andrew said. "I won't deny that, and I'm sorry to hear that he misrepresented why he wanted to meet you. On the other hand, there are mysteries in the world, Jenna, and the Church is familiar with many of them." He looked up at the painting of Mary, at the frame I'd just been poking at, and his familiar features suddenly seemed strange to me. His face, always so friendly and gentle, now looked almost suspicious. "If I were to hazard a guess, there are mysteries in your life that you are trying to unravel right now, yes?"

How much did Father Andrew know about all this, if anything? I wasn't sure, but now I wasn't sure if I could even trust him—or anyone else for that matter—right now. In the distant past, I had made confessions to him, but now wasn't the time or the place, even though I couldn't believe he knew anything for sure.

"I was just leaving," I said. My voice sounded odd and distant in my ears.

"You look a little pale, Jenna," he said. "Are you sure you're all right?"

I wanted to tell him I was perfectly fine, and to not worry about me, but the words got lost on their way from my brain to my mouth. I felt lightheaded and my breath was coming in short gasps. Father Andrew took my arm and gently guided me back to a pew and helped me sit down.

"Take a couple of deep breaths," he said. "You've had a tough few days." Outside the wind howled again. "And this strange weather is enough to make anyone nervous."

"I'm fine," I managed to say, forcing the words out. "Really."

"Would you like a glass of water?"

"No, nothing, thanks," I said. "I'll be fine." I managed to get my breathing under control and not sound like I'd just run a marathon.

"Well, after so many years of being a priest, I've tried to learn not to fuss over people who don't want to be fussed over." He smiled. "I'm not good at it, I admit, but I'm trying."

I smiled back at him. No matter what he did or didn't know, Father Andrew wasn't a threat to me or the Board. He was practically a member of the family. I realized that I hadn't taken the time to eat anything all day, so it was no wonder I was feeling a little woozy. Maybe my hunger was making me paranoid, too, since Father Andrew couldn't harm a fly.

"You really have gone through a lot, Jenna," he said, patting my arm. "You can't expect to recover instantly from a loss like this. Are you getting plenty of rest, giving yourself the time you need to grieve?"

I almost laughed aloud. Time to grieve? I had barely had time to breathe!

Father Andrew must have mistaken the look on my face for pain. "Jenna," he said in what I called his I'm-a-Priest-and-You-Should-Listen-to-Me voice. "I'm not going to give you a bunch of platitudes about how time heals all wounds and God's will and all that. Some people find that sort of thing comforting, but I don't think you would. Your grandfather was a wonderful man and the last of your family. Losing him must have hurt you deeply and it's going to take time to deal with."

"I know," I said, trying to keep my voice steady. I wished I could tell him that it wasn't just my grandfather's death bothering me, but the strange things going on in my life. It would feel good to open up to someone, but I'd already spilled my guts to Tom, and was starting to wonder if that had been a good idea—not because he might tell anyone, but what if Simon tried to come after him?

"You're strong enough to handle this," Father Andrew was saying. "Your grandparents, and even your parents, gave you what you need to carry on."

I hoped he was right, considering that the mysteries that had sprung up around my family were deepening by the hour.

"Now, my sermon is over. Would you like to come over the rectory for some tea?"

I cleared my throat. "No, thank you, Father. But I would . . . I would like to ask you a question."

"Of course," he said. "Anything."

"Did my grandmother . . ." My voice trailed off as I tried to figure out how to phrase what I wanted to know.

"Did she what?"

"Did she ever . . . I don't know . . . say anything strange to you? Anything at all?"

Father Andrew looked surprised. "Not that I can recall," he said. "About what?"

I sighed. "I don't know," I admitted. "I wish I did."

"Every family has its secrets, Jenna," he said. "You'll figure it out. Perhaps you should pray about it. Your grandparents were such stalwarts. I don't think they ever missed a Sunday, either one of them. And your grandmother did so much work in the garden here."

I nodded, getting to my feet and picking up my backpack again.

"The roses never bloomed half so well after she died," Father Andrew continued. "And your grandfather, too, was always fixing something around the church. Do you remember him repairing the pedestal of that statue? He worked so hard on the pedestal, getting the bricks just right."

And suddenly I did remember. My grandmother kneeling, her floppy straw hat on her head, the knees of her jeans black with potting soil. That was an image of her I'd carried with me all these years. The memory sharpened with thought . . . Grandmother was weeding and I was picking violets and blowing dandelion fluff. My grandfather was there, too, in the dirty, paint-splattered coveralls that he always wore when he was fixing something. He was shoring up the pedestal of Mary's statue with new bricks and fresh mortar. A statue in the garden.

Was Father Andrew trying to tell me something? I didn't know, but it seemed worth a try.

"Thanks for the talk, Father," I said. "Maybe I'll see you on Sunday."

"Maybe," he said, smiling. "Come by anytime, Jenna."

I quickly shook his hand, then turned and almost ran out of the church, anxious to get to the statue.

ST. ANNE'S. MOTHER MARY. 3rd FROM RIGHT. The words on the scrap of paper rang in my head as I cut across the half-frozen grounds to where the statue was placed. I felt an excitement brewing in my blood, and as I reached the statue, I slid to a stop, then knelt on the ground.

The third brick from the right . . . third from the right. My eyes roved over the pedestal, until I saw it. The mortar on the top layer was loose. I put my fingers in the grooves on either side of the brick and pulled.

It fell into my hand easily.

Behind it was a dark space, and I slipped my hand inside, wondering what I would find. The bricks and mortar were rough and damp on my skin. My fingers inched their way forward, skimming dirt, until I felt something slick and smooth—a plastic bag.

I pulled the bag out. It was a large Ziploc and inside was something wrapped in white cloth. Still kneeling next to the statue, I opened the bag, pulled out the bundle, and tugged the cloth loose. Inside was a book.

It felt too heavy for its size, almost as though it were made of stone instead of leather and paper. I glanced at the spine and the front cover, but there was no lettering on either surface. The pages curled slightly at the edges because of the damp and age, and on one corner, a dark stain, almost a deep brown, had soaked through the cover and into the pages below.

The cover felt soft and smooth to my fingers, and though it should have been cool to the touch after spending years hiding within the brick pedestal, it was as warm as the flesh of my hands. Briefly, the idea that there were veins and arteries swimming beneath the surface of the leather, that this book somehow pulsed with a life of its own, ran through my mind. I shuddered.

Out of the corner of my eye, I saw a glint of light and looked up to see one of the curtains in the rectory windows twitch. Perhaps it was Father Andrew walking by and he'd brushed the curtain with his shoulder . . . or maybe he really did know more than he was willing to let on. I wasn't sure.

It must be the excitement, I thought, of finding out that there really was a book. I was eager to look at it, to explore the pages within. I opened it and quickly saw that every page was handwritten—it was a journal!—but before I could begin to make sense of the words or decide where to start, I heard whispered voices coming my way.

I replaced the brick in the pedestal and shoved the book into my backpack, then stood up. On the other side of the gardens, three men with dark skin and long overcoats were looking around the grounds carefully.

Suddenly, one of them spotted me. "There she is!" he yelled.

For a moment, I had no idea what he was talking about, then I realized that he meant me! All three turned my way and began running toward me.

I stood there, frozen, and then Simon's words rang in my mind: *many people would willingly kill for it.* Was the Board what these strangers wanted? I took another look at the men coming my way and reached a decision. I didn't know for sure that it was the Board they wanted, but their intentions were definitely *not* friendly.

I turned and ran toward the parking lot and my car.

A voice shouted from behind me. "Cut her off!"

Looking up, I realized that there were several more men in the parking lot. I was trapped between the two groups and had nowhere to go.

I felt a sudden constriction in my chest, and wondered if anyone would hear me if I screamed for help or if Father Andrew still around? I clutched my backpack to my chest, spinning and trying to keep both groups of men in sight as they rushed toward me.

"We've got her. She's not going anywhere," one of the men said in a low voice.

Afraid, I wanted to scream or close my eyes. What had happened to my life? I just wanted to go back to the way things had been: my grandfather alive, going to college, drinking coffee with friends and thinking about my future as a cultural anthropologist.

Without warning, the winds sprang to life around me. The surge was so strong that it felt like a tornado had descended. I felt my hair fly up in all directions and the men slowed their approach.

A strange surge of cold electricity charged through my body, and I felt my backpack turn to ice. Then the wind lifted me off my feet and I felt myself floating through the air, held aloft like a magician doing a levitation trick.

"What the . . ." I had time to say aloud before I saw the ground rushing up to meet me. The gusting winds stopped as suddenly as they'd started, and I hit the pavement hard enough to jar my teeth. I rolled as I hit, clinging to my backpack.

I was on the other side of the group that had blocked me from my car. I didn't know how or why, and this was no time to stop and think about it. Thankful to be alive and free for the moment, I got to my feet and ran for my car.

I risked a glance behind me and saw the winds still swirling around my assailants. Dead leaves rose into the air in twisting columns, and I saw them struggling against the gusting breezes, trying to get to me.

I wished that I knew what they wanted for sure, but my instincts told me that at least in this, Simon had been telling the truth. They wanted the Board and were willing to do anything to get it. I had to get away.

Jumping into my car and throwing my backpack into the passenger seat, I saw that the winds had finally died down and the men were getting closer. I turned the key in the ignition and prayed that it would start as well as it had when I was trying to get away from Simon.

It did. The engine caught at once and roared to life.

I didn't hesitate, but slammed it into gear and floored the accelerator. My tires squealed as I pulled a tight circle in the parking lot, and I grimaced, knowing that I was leaving skid marks. Father Andrew would not be happy about that.

Torn between exhilaration and panic, I took off into the streets.

Two blocks later, I looked back to see if they were following me, but I saw no one. Still, I kept turning at random streets, left then right, not following any real direction. My hands were clenched on the steering wheel so hard that my knuckles had turned white.

Eventually, I realized that either they hadn't followed or I'd lost them. My heart rate finally slowed down and that's when I started shaking so hard I had to pull over and wait for my body to calm down.

There was nothing like being chased by thugs, I realized, to lend the mysteries of life a certain morbid depth. With this cheery thought came another. I didn't know who I could trust and what was really going on. My life was a mess, and all I wanted to do was go home and hide. Then I realized that home wasn't even safe.

For the first time since my grandfather's funeral, I started to cry.

"What do you mean you failed—again?"

"My Lord, this girl . . . she is already using the Board's powers, even untrained. She used the winds to escape our men."

"Did she? Using the Board is one thing, but controlling it is quite another."

"Also, our contact reached us. He claims to have been able to get in touch with her again."

"Find out when and where and if he fails this time, pick it up yourself. And don't lose her this time."

When my tears finally stopped, I pulled out my cell phone. For a minute, I sat there, wondering how to get in touch with Simon. I had to believe that even if he talked about things I didn't understand, he *knew* things I didn't. Instead, I speed-dialed Tom. If anyone besides Simon could help, it would be him.

He answered on the second ring. "Jenna," he said, as always, cheating with the caller-ID. "What's going on?"

I took a deep breath. "Tom," I said. "I think I need some help."

I could almost feel him switching gears. "No problem," he said, suddenly all business. "What do you need?"

"A place to crash for a while—a night anyway."

"You got it," he said. "When will you be here?"

"Fifteen minutes," I said. "I'll pick us up some coffee on the way."

"You're a wonderful woman and I forgive you for every mean thing you ever did to me." He paused, then added, "Except the time you tried to pull my hair out by the roots when we were in junior high."

I laughed weakly, but it was a real laugh nonetheless. "Thanks," I said. "I'll see you in a few."

"I'll be here," he said, then broke the connection.

I went by the coffee shop and headed over to Tom's apartment. He must have been watching for me because he opened the door before I could even knock.

"Come in," he said, taking his caramel latte out of my hand, and gesturing me inside. He shut the door behind me and locked it, then followed me into the living room.

As usual, his place was a chaotic mess of books, software packages, and computer equipment jammed onto shelves, the sofa, chairs, and his desk. I tossed my backpack on the floor at my feet, pushed several stacks of stuff out of the way, and then plopped down on the couch with a sigh. Tom's apartment was small and decorated like a typical college bachelor in scrounged garage sale furniture. I took a sip of my triple-shot mocha and realized that my mind was bouncing all over the place.

Tom sat down in a plush chair and sipped his own coffee appreciatively. His sandy brown hair would turn a golden shade of blonde in the summer, and sometimes when I looked at him, I could still see the young boy he used to be.

After a few minutes, he said, "Want to tell me what's going on?"

I thought about it and shook my head. How could I tell him when I didn't understand myself? "No," I said. "Not really. I'm not sure I'm ready to talk about it yet."

He nodded. "Fair enough," he said. "When you're ready, I'm here for you."

I smiled weakly at him. "I know, Tom. And you're a saint for giving me a place to crash. I think I just need to rest for right now."

"Happy to do it," he said.

Tom was my best friend, and wicked smart, too. I resolved that I would talk to him as soon as I had wrapped my own brain around what the Board was and why I was being chased for it.

"Thanks," I said. "I mean it."

"I know you do, Jenna," he said. "I'll follow where you lead—I always have, you know."

Both of us laughed, sharing a memory without having to speak it aloud. When we were kids, Tom was always the quiet one, smarter than I was and happy to do whatever I told him . . . like hide in the trunk of a broken down car. He'd been stuck there for hours waiting for someone besides me to find him.

"Listen," he said, "I'm supposed to be going out with Kristen tonight, but I can cancel if you need the company."

I shook my head. "No, I just want the quiet. You go ahead. Kristen would skin you alive for canceling a date with her to hang out with me."

"She *is* a little jealous," Tom admitted. "But . . . I kind of like it, too."

"We're *not* fighting over you, Tom," I said. "You're hers for the taking. I've got more problems right now than whom I'm going to date."

"I know," he said with a wistful smile, "but wishful thinking is a form of optimism."

"Is that so?" I asked. "Well, go right on being wishful, then . . . and go on your date."

"Okay," he said. "The bed is already made with fresh sheets. Why don't you crash in there tonight? I'll sack out on the sofa when I get home."

"You're very sweet . . . for a geeky nerd," I replied.

"That's me," he said. "Sweet, geeky nerd."

I laughed. "Get out of here and have a good time. I'm exhausted."

"No offense, but you look it," he said. I threw a pillow at him, which he dodged gracefully before getting to his feet and grabbing his coat. "You want me to call later and check in on you?"

"No," I said. "I plan to be sleeping like the dead by then."

"All right, catch you later, Jenna. Make yourself at home."

"Thanks again, Tom."

"You're welcome," he said, embracing me in a quick, warm hug, then quietly slipping out the door. I heard him lock it from the other side.

It was sweet that he hadn't pressed me for more information. Tom was like that—an interesting mix of smarts and common sense and decency all rolled into one package. Not for the first time, I wished I felt something for him other than that. He deserved it, but it wouldn't be right to try to feel something I didn't or to lie to him about it. I was content to have him as a friend, and even though I knew he would have liked more, I hoped he was happy with what we had as well.

I didn't have any clothing with me, but when I went into Tom's bedroom, I found that he'd already set out a clean T-shirt as well as two towels.

I made long use of the shower, then slipped into the T-shirt that was emblazoned with a giant picture of William Shatner as Captain Kirk from *Star Trek* along with the words INTERGALACTIC STUD. I grinned and put it on.

I curled up on the bed and pulled the Board and the journal out of my backpack. Setting the Board and its case aside, I opened the journal to the back. If it had been my grandmother's, the most recent entries would be there.

I gazed down at the page and blinked in confusion. I couldn't even begin to read the words. I hadn't even seen letters like these before. It wasn't English or even Latin text. I almost cried in frustration—the words were a lot like the symbols on the Board, meaningless to me. I didn't recognize any of it at all, and I felt both disappointed and angry. It wasn't fair.

The sting of tears ran across my vision and I swept a hand angrily over my face. I was *not* going to cry again. All I wanted was some information, a clue as to what was going on. I stared at the book, completely frustrated. *Help me!* I wanted to scream.

As I stared at the page, the indecipherable letters blurred, shifted, then cleared. I blinked, but they were perfectly readable now. The language was English, and with wonder, I looked at the top of the entry I had turned to:

The Chronicle of the Keepers, May 9, 1992—Margaret McKay Solitaire

My grandmother! Excited, I continued reading.

Our line is broken . . . my daughter, Moira, is dead and the trust must be passed on to my granddaughter, Jenna, though it is a poor inheritance I leave her.

But there must be a Keeper . . . without one, who will control the Board?

I have kept the Board safely hidden away, as my mother instructed me, and I have never used it. The temptation to do so has been strong, but I have been able to resist.

Moira was ready to take on the mantle—she was so strong and gifted . . . will Jenna have the same strength? Only time will tell.

My mind raced. As far as my grandmother and mother were concerned, the Board was real. A real *what* I didn't know, but questions filled my mind. Foremost among them was the question of who made the Board.

I'd no sooner had this thought, when I felt myself *pulled* away from Tom's apartment and into another place and time—a place and time where I was no longer me . . .

From the tower window, I see a still and flat land before me, an empty desert of baked earth and small scrub brushes flattened by wind. The sky is overcast, the reddish clouds above are thick and heavy. It is not sunset or sunrise, but the reflection of heat and flame. Part of the city beneath me is on fire and I suspect that whatever we have wrought has gone terribly wrong.

The tower is massive, soaring into the sky above the city like a gigantic arm thrust toward the heavens. It is made of clay bricks that mirror the dull color of the plains below. Behind me is a small, square worktable. I turn my attention back to my duties.

A mirror above the table catches the light and I see that my linen shift is stained with soot and something else . . . blood.

The symbols stitched into it, that mirror those on the Board set upon the table, are unmarked. The magic that preserves them still holds. I glance at my face in the mirror, and my tired eyes stare back at me. There is a flash of power in them and I know I can continue.

I must continue.

I pick up the long, curved dagger from the table, its point as vicious as a tiger's claw. I hold it carefully, poised over the Board. Just completed, the runes are sharp-carved into the rough surface, the wood branded with scorch marks and soot. The symbols are fresh and crisp.

It is ready to be awakened.

I am enthralled by this moment. Along with the others, I have worked so hard to create these items of Power, and in the currents of magical energy, I can tell that we have succeeded . . . and yet maybe we have failed. I do not know for certain, but to stop now would be the death of us all.

I hesitate, draw in a careful, steadying breath, and plunge the dagger into the wood surface. Something or someone screams, a noise that is everywhere yet nowhere at the same time. I continue to carve the final rune.

I realize that the sound is coming from the Board itself. It is alive. It is awake. And something . . . something dark and unsuspected has come into the Tower.

I draw the final line of the goat's head rune, and ignore the pounding on the door. "Shalizander!" a voice cries. It is rough and urgent. "Shalizander, stop!"

I cannot stop. I must finish. Too much of my energy has

JENNA SOLITAIRE

been put into this to end now. There is a flare of light beneath the door and it cracks, then splinters open. The door falls away from the hinges, and I manage to finish the last line without ruining it.

The room fills with birds—hundreds, perhaps thousands. Wings beat at the air and sharp beaks and claws tear at my clothing and the tapestries on the walls. I stumble away from the Board, keeping my hands up to protect my face.

The air is filled with the scent of feathers, and I scream, calling on the last vestiges of my strength . . .

There is darkness and the birds are gone. I rise from my knees, and grasp hands with the man kneeling next to me. "I'm sorry," he says. "I lost control of it."

He could be my twin, our skin is the same deep bronze, our hair the same onyx black. Only his eyes are different, a pale blue that shifts in the light.

"Do not be afraid," he says. "We have succeeded."

There is a mark burned into his face, across one cheekbone. It is the goat's head symbol with the horns. His burned flesh is an angry, red welt, yet he doesn't seem to be in any pain.

I want to believe him. I love him, and yet . . .

"What went wrong?" I ask.

"Nothing," he says. "Nothing is wrong, my love."

I want to believe him, but I don't. There is something foreign in his eyes and as I try to gather my courage, I know what it is. The dark presence I felt enter the Tower when I finished the Board is here . . . it is in him. But it wants more. It wants us all.

I stumble away from him, my mouth open to scream. That is when he starts laughing . . .

I sat up in Tom's bed, gasping, the vision—or had it been a dream?—so clear it was like watching a movie in my head. My head pounded and my stomach rolled. I put a hand to my forehead and rubbed my temple. I must have fallen asleep while reading the journal. It is on the bed next to me, closed, and in the other room, I heard Tom snoring away on the couch.

I looked at the clock next to the bed. It was almost nine in the morning! I realized that I'd been asleep for almost twelve hours. Confused, I would have sworn that I had only sat down on the bed a few moments ago. The vision or dream or . . . whatever . . . had lasted hours, not minutes.

From my backpack on the floor, I heard the beep of my cell phone telling me that I had new messages. Ignoring it for the moment, I got up and went into the bathroom, then turned on the coffeemaker that Tom had preset before going to sleep the night before.

The coffeemaker gurgled as it finished brewing, and I poured a cup and returned to the bedroom. I got my cell phone out of my pack and saw the little icon telling me I had one new message. I keyed the command to listen to it and heard Professor Martin's voice: "Jenna, I don't know what happened yesterday, but I did speak to that colleague of mine. He would love to see the Board and thinks he might be able to help you with some information on it. His name is Thaddeus Burke, and he owns a small antique shop downtown. I'll be there around ten this morning if you'd like to meet me with the Board."

There was a brief pause, then he added: "Jenna, I really am sorry about yesterday. I hope you let me help you. Artifacts like the one you've discovered are very unique and I'd love to have some small part in discovering its significance."

He added a quick address, then hung up.

I couldn't understand why I had reacted the way I did yesterday myself. I'd known Professor Martin for two years. He was a wonderful teacher and a good person. I had gone to him for help and then run out of his office like a terrified schoolgirl. I owed him an apology. Besides, if he had information about the Board, I *had* to go.

I glanced at the journal and decided not to look at it again for a while. I had hoped it would give me more information—a connection, maybe, to my mother or grandmother that I'd never had—but there was something disconcerting about reading it . . . like it had taken me into the dream I'd had the night before.

Still, at least now I knew that Shalizander was a name . . . almost like it was my own. In the dream, I *was* her.

I dressed hurriedly and scribbled a note for Tom. I left the journal hidden in the back of his bottom dresser drawer, but put the Board back in my pack, then slipped quietly out of the apartment. If I was going to make it on time, I couldn't wait for Tom to wake up. I'd talk to him later and tell him as much as I could.

Outside, I unlocked my car and climbed in, tossing my backpack into the passenger seat. Before I could key the ignition, someone appeared in the back seat.

I screamed and tried to jump out, but then heard Simon's quiet voice.

"Jenna. You need to listen to me."

"You . . . you . . ." I tried to find a word strong enough to express my feelings for this man who'd brought such confusion and chaos into my life, but nothing remotely polite came to mind. "What. Are. You. Doing. *IN MY CAR?*" I asked.

"Waiting for you," he said, shrugging. "It's a small town and there's only so many places you might be."

"Why?" I asked. "Why are you waiting for me? Did you spend the night in my backseat?"

"As a matter of fact, I did," he said. "It's not the most comfortable bed, but it was a safe bet that you'd show up here."

I sighed. "I'm late for an appointment, Simon. And if you don't stop harassing me, I'm going to call the police."

His eyes were tired, and for a moment he didn't speak. He reached up uncomfortably and touched his necklace. "Jenna, just listen. I'm not out to hurt you. I'm trying to protect you."

"From *what?*" I nearly screamed. "My biggest problem right now is you."

"What about those men who came after you at the church yesterday?" Simon asked.

"You saw that?" I said. "And didn't help me?"

"No, I didn't see it," he replied. "I was told. It's a small town, like I said." He put a hand on my shoulder. "Won't you let me help you, Jenna?"

He seemed sane enough, but I've found that all the crazy people usually do.

"Simon, get out of my car," I said. "I don't need or want your help. I just want my normal life back."

He climbed out of the car and shut the door. "You can't have your life back," he said. He looked almost sad. "You're a Keeper now."

"No, I'm a woman with an antique Monopoly board that I don't understand."

"If you let me help you, maybe you *can* understand."

I looked at my watch. "I've got to go, Simon. Maybe, maybe we'll talk later."

"Fine," he said. "Just remember what I told you. People will kill for it. You can't trust anyone when it comes to the Board."

"Not even you?" I asked.

"No," he said, his voice solemn. "Not even me." Then he turned and walked away.

Strangely, I felt sad to see him go. He was sincere, if nothing else.

I put the car in gear and headed for downtown. By lunchtime, I hoped to have some real answers about the Board and why my grandmother thought it was our sacred duty to keep it safe.

"My Lord, everything is well in hand. They've gone to Burke. I expect to have the Board shortly."

"Good, but I have another task for you. I want to see this girl who uses the Board so quickly. Bring them both to me."

Downtown Miller's Crossing consisted of a central square with a courthouse that had been renovated several years ago, and a number of small shops and banks on the other sides of the street. Parking was at a premium during the week, but on the weekends almost everybody did their shopping out at the mall, leaving the downtown area open.

I saw Professor Martin's car and pulled in to a space available next to it.

He got out of his car, holding a small box, and smiled. "Jenna! I hoped you'd come."

"Hi, Professor," I said, feeling sheepish. "I'm . . . well, I'm really sorry about yesterday. I don't know what came over me."

"It's okay," he said fondly. "You've had a lot on your plate these last few days. It's no wonder you're feeling stressed." He glanced at my backpack. "Did you bring the Board?" he asked.

I nodded. "Yes, and I see you've brought something, too."

He grinned. "Indeed." He opened the box and gestured inside. "Take a peek."

I did and grimaced. Inside was a tiny skull wrapped with beads and feathers. "What is it?" I asked.

"Romanian death curse," he said. "Very deadly. Certain to annihilate your worst enemies, or at the least give them a bad case of hives. I've been thinking of taking it to faculty meetings."

We both laughed.

"Actually," he said, "I brought it to have Burke authenticate it for me. He's very knowledgeable, and that's why I thought he could help you."

"I hope so," I said. "At this point, any information would be good."

"I imagine so," he said. "Let's go in and I'll introduce you."

I followed him onto the sidewalk while he continued to ramble on about Romania and a trip he planned on taking this summer to the Balkans to study their cultural magic. At any other time I would have found it fascinating, but not now. The dusty front window of Burke's shop had a shade drawn over it and a sign reading: OPEN BY APPOINTMENT ONLY. Another sign, reading CLOSED, hung from the door.

"Is he even here?" I asked, trying not to sound disappointed. The place looked as if it had been abandoned for years, and an alley running along one side of the building was littered with trash and debris.

"Of course," Professor Martin said. "*We* have an appointment." He opened the door and gestured for me to enter the dark interior, then shut and locked it behind us. I must have looked startled, because he shrugged and said, "He told me to lock it up as we came in."

I nodded and looked around. Shabby table and chair sets that didn't look much older than I was, candlesticks that didn't match, battered jewelry spread out on a chipped, painted tray. Junk and more junk.

This was the antique shop of someone who could help me?

"Not everything is as it appears, Jenna," Professor Martin said, leading me further into the shop. He gestured around. There were still cheap antiques scattered on tables and heaped on shelves and in corners, but there were also displays of crystals set into necklaces and bracelets, strange stones or gems in bowls. Candles and incense and packs of tarot cards with different styles of painting. Jars of dried herbs. Tiny glass vials filled with powders and dark liquids.

Books without titles on the spines and some with titles that indicated New Age metaphysical nonsense.

"This stuff is for tourists, Jenna," Professor Martin explained. "The real goods are kept safely locked away in the back for people who know what they're searching for. Trust me, Burke really knows what he's talking about." He glanced toward the back of the shop and called out, "Burke!"

As we reached the back counter, a man stepped out from behind a beaded curtain that hung over the doorway leading to the storage areas of the shop. My first thought was that he didn't fit his environment at all. I expected someone with a ponytail and a crystal earring dangling from his lobe, barefoot or wearing Birkenstock sandals, and grinning like a fool while happily telling me how I could heal cancer by visualizing myself surrounded by a glowing, white light. Someone Kristen would have felt comfortable spending time with. What I saw instead was a short man with burly shoulders and close-cropped, dirty black hair. The grumpy expression on his face looked permanently etched there.

"Martin," he said. "You said you've got something to show me?"

"I do," he said, setting his box down on the counter. "A Romanian death curse."

"Yeah, right," Burke said. "And in back, I've got the Hope Diamond."

"You can look at mine in a minute, but first I want you to meet one of my students." Professor Martin put his hand on my back and gently pushed me forward. "This is Jenna Solitaire," he said. "It's her item that I called you about."

"Let's see it," Burke demanded. "Martin's got an imagination, you know, and I don't like wasting my time with stupidity."

For some reason, I hesitated. The store, the run-down alley beside it, the impatient, almost hungry look in Burke's eyes as he waited for me to show him the Board—all of it worked together to make me want to stammer an excuse and leave . . . just like I had in Professor Martin's office. It didn't make any sense, and I pushed the desire to run out of my mind.

I was being silly and paranoid, and it would be stupid to walk away from a potential source of information that Professor Martin recommended. He thought Burke might know something, and if he did, I *needed* to know it, too.

I pulled my backpack off my shoulder and slowly opened the zipper. Just as I reached inside, Burke interrupted me. "Not out here," he said.

He gestured for us to come behind the counter and pushed the beaded curtain aside. "In the back," he said.

The back room was dimly lit, with a single, bare bulb overhead. A thin man with a ratlike face—narrow and greedy and lacking a chin—was wrapping up a box with packing tape on a table in the corner.

"Tanner," Burke said. "Go out and watch the shop for a minute."

"I was just finishing this—" the man started to say.

"*Now,*" Burke said.

Tanner stalked out of the room, sniffling and wiping his nose on his sleeve. I barely paid him any attention, however, as the items stacked on the shelves here had caught my attention.

Some of the stock was just more of the same that was out front, but there were also other things. One jar on a shelf to my left looked like it was full of tiny hands, withered and dry and small as a baby's. Maybe they were monkey paws—if they were even real. The jar next to it was filled with waxy looking eyeballs that were surely made of plastic, although they looked real enough that I couldn't be quite sure. And there were books, too. Hundreds of volumes that were much, much older than the ones out front. Many of them were bound in leather and looked valuable. On one shelf, a pile of black candles rested next to a row of human skulls, yellowed and cracked with age. Some were missing their lower jawbones and rested unevenly on their teeth.

Waaay creepy, I thought.

Burke motioned to the table where Tanner had been working. "So, let's see what you've got," he said. His voice held a note of weary boredom.

Professor Martin stood next to me, his eyes alight with excitement. He'd already seen the Board and believed it to be special. I pulled the case out and set it on the table, then opened it gingerly and lifted out the Board.

Professor Martin grinned, but Burke's face didn't even flinch.

"Yeah?" he said. "So what?" He bent forward and looked at the Board indifferently, but I noticed that he didn't touch it, only skimmed one oddly delicate finger near one of the symbols, a breath above the surface of the wood. "This is it?" he asked.

Disappointed, I nodded. After Professor Martin's reaction and seeing the journal, I assumed the Board was something truly unique. Maybe my whole family had been caught up in some kind of hoax. Professor Martin seemed surprised, too.

"That's *it*? Don't you think—"

"I think a lot," Burke snapped. "More than you do anyway. I see a lot of stuff in this business. People find crap in their attic all the time, bring it in here hoping it's worth something, and it's still crap. I tell them all the time that this isn't the *Antiques Roadshow*."

I felt my face growing hot. I wasn't interested in money, just information. I cleared my throat. "I didn't really have any idea that it was worth something. I just wondered what it was, where it came from is all."

"Just so you don't get your hopes up," Burke said, bending back over the Board, frowning, and putting his nose near the wood surface.

"Take a look at those symbols," Professor Martin said. "Have you—"

He fell silent, cutting himself off in mid-sentence as Burke straightened up.

"I can probably find out something," Burke said to me, ignoring the professor. "Leave it here for a day or two and I'll do some digging, make a couple of phone calls and see what I can come up with. All right?"

I must have looked uncertain because Professor Martin quickly reassured me. "It will be fine, Jenna," he said. "Burke really does know more than anybody about . . . antiques."

Was it my imagination, or had Professor Martin paused just slightly before that last word?

"If there's anything to find out about the Board, Burke is the man to find it," Professor Martin continued.

I nodded and wrote down my name and phone numbers on a slip of paper, which I handed to Burke, still trying to force myself not to grab the Board and run like a terrified rabbit.

Professor Martin held open the beaded curtain doorway for me and I started to step through, but stopped and looked back at Burke. He was easing the Board back into its case, holding it delicately by the edges so his short, blunt fingers never touched the surface itself.

I was almost through the curtain when I felt a peculiar wrench inside, as if something had just grabbed hold of one of my intestines and squeezed. I gasped for air, remembered having this same sensation when Professor Martin asked for me to leave the Board with him.

I couldn't leave it then, and I can't do it now. I know I can't.

Before I even took the time to think, I spun around and ducked past Professor Martin. I snatched the Board case out of Burke's hands.

"I, umm, I can't," I said, realizing that my brain was struggling to find words to explain my actions. "I just, you know, have to think about it. I promised to show it to some friends. Now, I mean, tonight. I better take it with me." I started backing away from Burke. "Maybe you can call me if you find out anything about it," I stammered, "and I'll . . . I'll bring it back."

Burke looked angry. "What the hell?" he muttered, glaring at Professor Martin. "You said she'd leave it."

"Jenna," Professor Martin said. "What's gotten into you? Are you sure you want to carry that around? It might be valuable, historically if not in terms of money. Why don't you leave it here and—"

"No!" I yelled, shocked by the loudness of my own voice. Trying to calm myself, I said, "I'd better go." I shoved the board case into my backpack and clung to it tightly, then turned and headed back to the front of the store, moving past Tanner who sat doodling on a stack of papers and gave me a funny look as I brushed past him.

"Jenna, wait!" Professor Martin called.

I stopped, knowing I must look like an idiot.

He put his hand on my arm. "Is everything all right?" he asked.

I felt myself blushing. "Fine," I said weakly. "I'm fine."

"Really, Jenna," he said. "Why don't you just leave the board with Burke? If you really want to find out more about it . . ."

His voice was kind and concerned but once again I could

see something in his eyes that was a little too eager and hungry. He stretched out a hand toward my backpack as though he was going to take it from my arms, but I stepped backward and when I looked in his eyes, the hunger was gone. Maybe I had imagined it.

"I've got to go, Professor," I said, and I turned around and headed for the front door to leave the shop. My heart was hammering away in my chest and I paused at the door and unlocked it, then slipped outside, expecting someone to grab me at any second and demand the Board. I must be going crazy, I thought. I passed by the alleyway as I headed back to my car when I saw the man standing in the shadows.

It was as if he had been waiting for me. The light was dim and the alley was dark and filled with shadows. I couldn't see him well, just a general impression of height, dark hair and a long, black trench coat. He wasn't walking, but simply stood there with his hands in his pockets, staring at me.

I suddenly *knew* who he was. The stranger at my grandfather's funeral. The man who had broken into my house.

Yet *another* mystery in my life. Another thing I didn't understand.

That is it! I thought. *I can't take another second of this.* The wind suddenly increased and reminded me that between the weather, the dreams, the whispers and all the strangers and people accosting me, I had reached my limit. This wasn't my life.

I wanted explanations and answers and all I got was more questions.

"Hey!" I shouted at the man. I stepped into the mouth of the alley. "Who are you?"

The man didn't answer me, just stood there staring.

"Answer me!" I yelled. "Who *are* you?"

I started to run into the alley, but someone grabbed my arm from behind, and used my own momentum to swing me around. I ended up on my knees on the brick surface of the alley. My backpack flew out of my hands and landed in a puddle. My brain briefly registered an image of two feet clad in grubby white running shoes standing next to my pack, and then a hand in a brown glove reaching down and grasping one of the straps.

I yelled, throwing myself forward and grabbing at it with both hands. I tried to ignore the cold, muddy puddle I landed in, and simply held on. I couldn't let this person— whoever he was—get away with the Board. Yanking myself backward, I swung my body around and began flailing with my feet, landing a solid kick to the mugger's knee.

He swore and staggered back a step. Looking up, I saw that his face was covered by a black ski mask and he held a short-bladed knife in one hand.

"Come on!" he said. "Just give the darn thing up." His voice was thin, with a nasal whine to it as though he thought he deserved the Board for all his hard work.

Giving up the Board was not an option. I scrambled to my feet, yanking my backpack into my arms. The mugger waved the knife threateningly and I stepped to one side. He tracked me with his eyes and the blade of the knife.

I leaped to one side, trying to get around him and get into the relative safety of the street, but my foot slipped on a patch of mud and I fell to my knees. The mugger grabbed at my shoulder and I had no trouble at all imagining his knife at my throat.

Instinct kicked in and I shut my eyes, hunching over the backpack, hugging it close to my chest. A gust of wind chased down the alley and blew the hair over my face.

Behind me, I heard a sharp grunt, a crash and a clatter and the mugger's hand fell away from my shoulder. I shook the hair out of my eyes and looked up to see my attacker sprawled on the ground a few feet away, a trash can lying next to him that he'd knocked over in his fall. Standing over him with his back to me was the man I'd seen staring at me from the alley.

He took a step forward and made some kind of gesture with one hand. The alley was dark and I couldn't see very well, but it certainly alarmed the mugger, who got awkwardly to his feet and ran off down the alley, limping and splattering his way through the puddles on the ground.

I got back to my feet, still clinging to my backpack and wincing a bit as I put weight on my right leg. The knee of my jeans was torn and blood oozed from a scrape.

"Thanks," I said, hearing the shaking of my voice and hating it. I hated feeling or sounding weak. "Really, I—"

The man swung around to face me. *"What have you done?"* he demanded.

I didn't understand, and started to explain this. "I don't—"

He closed the gap between us and seized my arm. Hard enough to hurt.

"It has been awakened," he said angrily. "The wind, the weather—everything proclaims this to be true. How dare you betray your sacred trust?"

What is going on here? I wondered. The guy saves me from a mugger one minute and yells at me the next and for what? *I don't understand what it is he thinks I've done.*

I yanked my arm out of his grasp. "I don't know what you're talking about," I insisted. He grabbed my arm again—he had a grip like iron—and I yelped. "Hey! Let me go!"

He ignored me and dragged me closer, pulling my face up to his. "Who do you *serve?*" he asked.

We stared at each other for a few breathless moments. My heart was pounding away, adrenaline thundering through my veins . . . and yet, I felt strangely distant from these events. It was just another crazy man threatening me, asking me questions or trying to tell me things that made little or no sense. I hadn't even had time to call the police and this time there was no Simon around to chase away the bad guys. The mugger seemed like a minor threat—he'd just wanted my backpack. I didn't know what this man wanted.

I watched as the expression on the man's face changed from anger to puzzlement. "You do not understand?" he asked, clearly amazed by the idea. "You do not know?"

"No," I said. "I don't know."

"Then you must come with me—" he started to say.

"Jenna!" Professor Martin's voice called from the end of the alley.

Before I could answer, the man let go of my arms and I stumbled away from him. By the time I caught my balance again, Professor Martin was running down the alley toward me and the man in the black coat was gone.

"What was that all about?" the professor asked me as he escorted me back toward the street.

"I'm not sure," I said, still trying to figure it all out myself.

"Maybe you should talk to the police," he said.

I shook my head. The mugger was long gone and the man in the black coat . . . I didn't think he'd meant me any real harm. "I'm all right," I said as we reached my car.

"If you say so," Professor Martin said. "Are you sure you don't want to leave the Board with Burke? I really think he could help you."

"I'm sorry, Professor," I said. "I can't."

"All right," he said, the disappointment clear in his voice. "I've got to go, but I'll see you on campus, okay?"

"Sure," I said, just wanting to get back to Tom's apartment and hide. Everyone seemed to be acting strangely—even me—and I wanted to have a chance to sort things out.

The professor ran to his car, jumped in, and pulled out of the space. I watched him go, wondering why he was in such a rush, then shrugged. I hadn't met a professor yet that was completely normal—I'd been in college long enough to know that was a undeniable fact.

Just as I began to open the door to my own car, I heard

shuffling footsteps behind me. I whirled around, determined to face whoever this was head on.

A guy with a baseball cap pulled low over his eyes approached me. "Got the time?" he asks, his voice gruff and low.

I felt my shoulders sag with relief. "Sure," I said, looking at my watch. "It's—"

As I looked down at the ground, the man shifted his weight, favoring one leg as if it was sore.

That's when I knew his voice was familiar . . . and something dark, thick and heavy was pulled down over my face.

*"It's all arranged, my Lord. We'll take both her
and the Board from him at the airport, and both will
be in your hands within twelve hours."*

"You have done well, Peraud. I am not displeased."

"What of Burke and his associate?"

*"They have delivered where your contact could
not. Pay them as arranged. Burke knows his place.
There is no need to end a perfectly agreeable business
relationship."*

I tried to yell for help, but any sound I made was muffled by
the cloth over my face. Strong hands grabbed my arms and
pulled me away from the car, squeezing me tightly, even
through my coat and sweater. I twisted and writhed against
my new assailant, and felt my backpack fall out of my hands.

The Board! It might break when it hit the concrete.

I thrashed, trying to break free—not so I could escape, but
so I could pick up the Board again. I couldn't see, could

hardly breathe. An arm went across my chest, another around my throat and I felt my feet leave the ground. I tried to fight with everything I had when I felt a sharp pain in my right shoulder, a pinprick stabbing me.

My struggles weakened almost immediately, and I felt my arms and legs turn to lead. My muscles wouldn't respond and it felt like I was melting, turning into liquid and for a moment, I wanted to cry again.

All I could think about as I sank into the darkness was that I was going to lose the Board forever.

I drifted back into awareness and my first thought was that I had been buried, deep in the earth, like my grandfather. Buried *alive*. A weight pressed down on every inch of me, gluing my eyes shut, filling my mouth and my nostrils.

It was so heavy, and my body ached with the need to move, to scream, to turn around, to . . . do something to proclaim that I was still a living·human.

I wondered if I was having yet another dream or vision and I thought about how my grandfather would have comforted me . . . but he couldn't now. He was dead and this thought stirred my brain into waking. *My grandfather is dead and I'm not. I'm not buried and I have to figure out what has happened to me and protect the Board.*

I told myself to wake up—and then I did.

Being awake wasn't much better, I found, than being trapped in a dream. I tried to open my eyes, but something—tape, maybe—had sealed them shut. There was a thick cloth gag in my mouth and spitting it out was impossible. A vibrating noise that I didn't immediately recognize filled the air around me.

I realized that the drug I'd been injected with was still affecting my senses, and I waited a while longer to see if the effects would lessen. Eventually, I knew that I was lying on the dirty backseat floor of a car. In the front seat, I could hear voices speaking in harsh tones.

One was thin, sharp and angry, with a familiar high-pitched, nasal tone. "I don't like this, Burke. This is way further than we've gone before." The voice belonged to Tanner.

"Yeah, well, this is way bigger than anything we've ever handled before," Burke replied.

I immediately knew I was in real danger. These men had kidnapped me and I felt fear swirl in my stomach like an angry snake. Nausea rose in my belly and I thought for a second I might actually have to throw up. I swallowed hard to keep it from happening—with the gag in place, I would have suffocated. . . . I shuddered, trying not to think about it, wondering instead what Burke and Tanner intended to do with me.

"This is a lot of trouble," Tanner was saying. "Kidnapping is no joke."

"Will you stop whining?" Burke snapped. "It's only real trouble if we're caught and why should we get caught? The only people who know about this are you, me, Martin and that girl back there—and she's not going to be telling anybody."

I struggled against the ropes that they had used to tie my hands, to spit out the gag . . . but nothing worked. I was trapped, and frightened, but I also felt another emotion: anger. They'd taken the Board from me, lied to me, and they were sitting up there discussing me like last week's garbage to be taken out to the dump. I held onto the anger—it was the only useful emotion I'd felt so far. Anger would serve me better when the time came for action.

I twisted my hands, trying to loosen the ropes, hoping to get free.

"This is worth a little risk," Burke continued. "There are people out there who will pay serious money for that piece of wood. It's going to set me up for a long, long time."

I jerked, almost getting into a sitting position. He was talking about selling the Board! But if they knew I was awake, they wouldn't keep talking, so I forced myself to remain still.

The panic I felt at the idea of being parted from the Board was unnatural. I'd only had it for a few days, yet the very thought of losing it made my breath catch in my throat. I couldn't let them have it—it belonged to me.

The Board was mine.

Suddenly, I somehow knew that the Board was on the backseat above me. I couldn't explain how I knew that, but I did. It was almost like I could see it with another set of eyes. It was there and safe for the moment.

I tried to relax and listen to their conversation.

"You?" Tanner said. His voice was so nasty it felt like ants crawling on my skin. "You sent me out there to grab the girl

and her pack, do all the dirty work, and it's going to set *you* up for a long time?"

"Listen, Tanner," Burke said. "If you'd gotten her pack the first time, we wouldn't be having any trouble now. So shut the hell up."

Tanner grumbled something under his breath and Burke said, "What?"

"You didn't tell me she had some kind of bodyguard," he complained.

"Will you shut up about the so-called bodyguard? Did anybody try to stop us when we grabbed her at her car?"

"I'm telling you, this guy was creepy. There was something—"

"Just shut up, Tanner," Burke said. "I'm tired of hearing it."

There was silence for a moment, and then Tanner said, "What about Martin? He's going to want a cut."

"Yeah, but he doesn't know what he's got here. Not for sure. I'll give him a finder's fee like I usually do, a couple of thousand. Don't worry about him. We've worked together in the past."

My heart lurched in my chest. Professor Martin worked with Burke . . . he'd known about this. That was why he'd been in such a hurry to get away from the shop—in fact that was why he'd brought me to the shop in the first place! So much for not trusting my instincts, I vowed to myself. The hunger in Professor Martin's eyes was for money.

I tried to calm my ragged breathing and focus on listening to the two men in the front.

"I don't mind helping you find a buyer," Tanner said. "That's what I do. But I'm not helping you kill anybody or whatever it is you're planning."

"Since when did you become a girl scout?" Burke asked. I felt the car turn a sharp corner and I slid back against the seat, paper rustling around me. "Listen," he continued. "I'm not a pervert and I'm no murderer. Nothing's going to happen to the girl. Look at her back there, sleeping like a baby. She's fine. All she's going to think is that she got mugged—that's it. Pretty little girl like that should know better than to walk around town all by herself. So you can stop whining."

"Fine," Tanner said. "Then I guess you don't need me anymore tonight."

Burke slammed on the brakes and the car screeched to a halt. "You want to walk home, be my guest," he said.

I heard a car door open, and then slam shut. The vehicle lurched into motion again, and I wondered where Burke was taking me and what was going to happen when we got there. If he'd wanted me to think I'd been mugged, why drag me away from town?

I kept working at the rope around my wrists, trying to hold on to my anger while fear crept back into my mind. I couldn't afford to panic. My grandfather taught me that panic is what will get you killed, so *think* first. I could almost hear his voice in my head.

Burke had told Tanner that he didn't plan to kill me. He had the Board, so killing me didn't make any sense. Lost in thought, I barely noticed when the road surface changed from asphalt to dirt. The ping of gravel on the underside of the car rattled in my ears. Several minutes passed before the car slowed to a stop.

I heard Burke get out and his door shut. In the distance, I could hear the sound of running water, and guessed that we were near the river. Miller's Crossing had once been a trading post, and in the summer, plenty of people still used the waterway for kayaking, canoeing or fishing . . . but in the winter and early spring, it was deserted. No one would be anywhere nearby.

The door closest to my head opened, and I felt hands grasp my shoulders and pull me out of the vehicle. I tried to stay still and limp. It would be better if Burke still thought I was asleep and drugged. The element of surprise might be my only chance to escape.

My head and torso came out first, and my feet, still tied together at the ankles followed as Burke tugged at me. I felt them hit the ground with a thud, and then almost let out a gasp as I was hoisted into the air.

"Sorry about this," Burke muttered, panting with the effort of carrying my dead weight on his shoulder. "It's a waste, really, because you're a nice-looking young girl. But I can't have any loose ends and even though the man said he wanted you and the Board, I'm not going to take that kind of risk."

I suddenly knew that Burke had lied to Tanner. He wasn't going to leave me somewhere and let me wake up, thinking I'd been mugged.

He was going to kill me!

I thrashed and twisted wildly, yanking at the ropes that bound my hands together, but I couldn't get free. Burke was surprised by my sudden movement, however, and he grunted and dropped me to the ground. I didn't want to die, and as I felt a wooden surface beneath me, I did the only thing that came to mind . . . I rolled, and kept rolling.

In fact, I couldn't stop myself.

I felt the ground drop out from beneath me and a momentary weightlessness took me by surprise. The air was cold and I would have screamed, but the gag kept me silent, wailing to myself.

Then I hit the icy river, breaking through a skin of ice on the surface.

March in Ohio isn't spring, and the water cut at my body like a thousand tiny knives.

My nose filled with water, and the rag in my mouth was soaked in seconds. My coat soaked through and its weight began pulling me down to the river bottom.

I couldn't swim, couldn't see, and had no idea even which direction the surface might have been. Blinded, helpless, gagging . . .

The last moments of my life were passing in front of my eyes. These last days hadn't been fair or sane and all I wanted was to scream and cry, but the water was too cold, the gag choking me.

I knew I was going to die, drowned in the river and soaked in mud.

I expected to feel an icy grip, a burning maybe, as my lungs filled with the silty water and my death approached.

I expected to die, swallowing water and wishing I'd been smart enough to trust my instincts about Professor Martin and Burke. Wishing I still had the Board.

Death was coming for me. I knew it with every bone and fiber in my body.

But it didn't.

The water around me bubbled and surged and though I could feel it in my nose and my mouth . . . in my lungs . . . I did not die. I didn't even struggle for air.

My lungs expanded and contracted like always, but instead of dying, I was . . . I was breathing. I was breathing water! The miraculous nature of my survival was stunning and yet . . . it felt perfectly normal, like I had been breathing underwater my whole life. I stopped struggling and let myself sink.

I thought of the Board and almost at once, I could feel it as though it was in my hands. A voice, sibilant and almost hissing, whispered in my mind. *"Call to me and I am yours—the power of the Winds, of breath and life . . . you are the Keeper of the Winds."* I should have been frightened, but instead I felt only a sense of inner peace and calm, like I was being cradled in a protective bubble where nothing could hurt me.

I wondered if I was imagining the strange voice, then realized that sitting on the river bottom was no place to be thinking about things. Even if I didn't drown, the cold could kill me, too.

Whatever was happening, I had to get out of the water, fast. *Then* I could take time to puzzle things out. At least I wasn't dead and if I had the Board to thank for that, I'd gladly shower it with kisses . . . as soon as I got it back from Burke.

Slowly, I tugged at the ropes around my wrists. I had managed to loosen them a little earlier, and now I managed to stretch the ropes out even more. Blinded, my eyes squeezed tightly shut against the sting of the frigid water leaking over my tape blindfold, I drifted along the bottom. My sense of time was muted, as though it had ceased to really matter.

Finally, I got my stiff hands free and yanked the tape off my eyes and the gag out of my mouth. I saw the surface of the river above me, and I kicked with my ankles, feeling how lethargic my muscles already were in the freezing cold.

I didn't dare take the time to try and get the rope off my feet . . . I might not be able to drown, but I was pretty certain I could still freeze to death. I moved toward the surface, coated in muck and heavy with icy water in my clothes. I saw the bubbles of my breath floating up toward the surface ahead of me.

When I broke into the air, I coughed once, spitting water, and then drew air—sweet, regular air—into my lungs. The water clung to my clothing and the ropes binding my feet made kicking and swimming almost impossible. I reached down and managed to slip my feet out of my hiking boots *and* the ropes. I let them sink to the bottom.

My teeth were chattering from the cold and my legs were growing weaker by the second. I knew I couldn't swim much longer, and I felt the first stabbings of genuine panic that I might not be able to get out of the water.

The irony of being able to breathe underwater yet still die in the river wasn't lost on my half-frozen mind. In the failing light of the evening, I saw a wooden dock jutting out over the water, and thrashed my way toward it.

That must have been what I'd fallen off of when Burke dropped me.

I splashed toward the dock, shivers racing through my aching legs and my teeth chattering away like a child's wind-up toy. As I got closer and managed to snag a piling, I saw a man sitting on the top of the dock, calmly watching me struggle in the water.

"Help!" I tried to shout, but my voice came out as a quiet croak. I tried again. *"Help!"* That was better.

The man didn't appear to be in any hurry and the fact that he was obviously warm and dry made me even madder. For a moment, I wondered if it was Burke, returning to finish me off. He calmly lowered himself to the dock and stretched out flat, offering me his hand. In the shadows, I couldn't make out his features, but I didn't care. Help, even slow help, was better than nothing at all.

Exasperated and wrung out, I did my best to get my arms

up high enough for him to grab on to. Several times, my wet hands slipped out of his grasp, and once, I nearly pulled him into the river with me. I heard a muffled curse, and then he got a solid, desperate grip on my arms, and pulled me out of the water. I landed on the dock like a dying fish, my breath rasping in my lungs.

I watched as Simon Monk stood up and brushed off his hands. He frowned down at me, then reached out and lifted me to my unsteady feet.

I couldn't believe it, but it was even colder *out* of the water. I shivered uncontrollably as I stared at Simon, trying to find words and discarding them just as quickly.

Finally, I managed to spit out, "What took you so long?" The words were awkward and choppy between my chattering teeth, but they were clear enough.

He looked at me thoughtfully, and then he said, "I knew the Keeper couldn't drown."

"No? But I could sure freeze to death! Did you think of that?"

Simon slipped off his coat and wrapped it around my shoulders. "I did," he admitted. "But I figured if you were half-frozen it *might* slow you down enough that you would at least listen to me for once."

I knew I must have looked like a drowned, red-haired rat.

"Well," I said, trying unsuccessfully to control my shivering, "if you have a car with a heater, I'll sit in it long enough to get warm and listen to you at the same time."

"That's good enough for me," Simon said. "Wait here and I'll bring the car up to the dock."

He turned and walked away into the darkness and that's when I remembered the dream I'd had of drowning . . . the way the water outside the castle had felt when I had plunged in and hadn't died.

I felt my eyes roll back in my head, my knees wobbled and unlocked, and then I fell into the familiar darkness of unconsciousness.

"Wake up, Keeper . . ."

"No . . . I don't want to. It's warm here."

"Wake up, Keeper. You need to move around or you'll freeze to death. I cannot move your blood, but only the winds."

"I'm sleeping . . . leave me be."

"KEEPER! WAKE UP!"

"Why?"

"We have winds to call. The world turns and yet you sleep. My power will strengthen you, but only if you wake up."

"Winds to call?"

"Yes . . . with me, you can ride them like a Queen of the Air."

"Ride the winds?"

"Yes, Keeper. With me, you will rise above the houses and into the heavens themselves if you wish."

"I'm tired. I want to sleep more. I don't want to think any-more."

"I will give your thoughts wings. My power will be yours, but you must wake up."

"I don't want to."

"You must."

"I am afraid."

"I will protect you."

"You will?"

"Always. You can trust me."

"Then yes."

"My Lord . . . Burke and his man claim the girl escaped."

"And?"

"Unfortunately, I believe him. He does, however, have the Board."

"That is fortunate—for his sake. Your one task—your only task now—is to find the girl. Use whatever means are necessary, but I want her almost as much as I want the Board."

"Jenna, wake up!"

I tried to peel open my eyelids, but I was so tired and sleep was so warm.

"Jenna, wake up. Wake up right now!"

I felt someone slapping lightly at my face. "No," I grumbled. "Don't want to."

"I know you don't want to, but you have to," the voice said. "Come on now."

The voice was nice. Deep, masculine and commanding,

127

yet compassionate, too. Not like the sibilant voice in my dream that wanted me to wake up and made promises of winds and power. More light slaps tingled on my face, and I finally managed to open my eyes.

Simon was bent over me, his handsome features furrowed with concern. Everything came back to me in a rush—I was lying on a dock that stretched out over the half-frozen river. Where I had discovered that I could breathe underwater, but that freezing to death was still possible. Where I'd lost the Board.

The Board!

The thought snapped me into full wakefulness.

"Oh, God," I said, groaning as thousands of pins and needles of cold stabbed my body. "The Board—it's gone."

"I know," Simon said. He hauled me to my feet. "Let's get you into the car and warmed up."

Without a word or sound of complaint, he picked me up and carried me to his rented sedan. I buried my face on his shoulder, feeling his strength and smelling his clean scent . . . and wishing I hadn't. This was *not* a man I wanted to be attracted to.

Simon opened the passenger door and helped me climb in. The heater was already running at full blast and the hot currents of air washing over me felt wonderful. I leaned back into the seat gratefully as Simon climbed in the driver's side.

"Better?" he asked.

I nodded. "Much. Thank you."

"Good," he said. "Now, maybe you'll do me the kindness of at least *listening* to what I have to say?"

"Yes," I said, already thinking back to my amazing experience on the river bottom and knowing that whatever had allowed me to survive drowning had to be connected to the Board and Simon.

Simon nodded. "Very well. The first thing you must understand, Jenna, is that the Board is *not*, as I've tried to tell you, a child's toy. It is an ancient artifact, dating back to at least before the time of Christ and maybe much longer than that."

"From before the time of Christ," I said, thinking of the Tower and the red plains beyond it.

"Yes," he said. "But there is much more. The Board is, beyond a doubt, a magical item of true power. Based on the research I've done, the Solitaire line of women have been the Keepers of the Board for many hundreds of years—perhaps since it was first created." Simon turned and stared directly at me. "And as you've already learned, there are people who will stop at nothing to possess it. Its value is incalculable."

When I didn't say anything, Simon added, "Jenna, I'll tell you again, these people will gladly *kill* for it. Do you understand that?"

Trying to keep a rein on my temper, I said, "I think my kidnapping and swim in the river makes that pretty obvious, don't you?"

"Sarcasm isn't going to help us much at this point."

"Us?" I said. "There is no 'us.' There's me. Alone. Hence the name Solitaire."

"Jenna—" he began.

"No," I said. "I can't take another minute of this . . . this . . . whatever it is. I don't want to be the Keeper, I didn't ask to be the Keeper. And I don't believe in magic! There has to be some other explanation." I realized that my voice had risen to almost a shout, and I tried to control it.

"I just want my life back the way it was before all this craziness."

"I'm sorry, Jenna," Simon said. "But that isn't an option based on my research of the Boards. Being the Keeper is your destiny and you must accept it now, before more things spin out of control."

"Would you stop telling me about your research?" I yelled. "The Board's gone now anyway. If you want it, go track down Burke yourself and take the thing."

Even as I said this, a part of me still felt the Board's loss, and my longing for it, almost a physical need. What was happening to me?

"It doesn't work that way," he said. "Besides, only a fool who wasn't the Keeper would even touch the thing, let alone use it. The repercussions would be . . ." He didn't finish his sentence as his gaze went out the window. During our conversation, the winds had risen again, and the trees along the riverbank were bent over, their branches popping and cracking.

Simon turned back to me. "Jenna . . . tell me you didn't attempt to *use* the Board!"

I could hear the fear in his voice, and didn't respond right away, but stared out the window instead. The sun had disappeared and the moon was hidden behind heavy clouds, enveloping us in thick darkness. The interior of the car was illuminated only by the dashboard lights, lending an eerie green glow to Simon's face, and mine too, no doubt. Suddenly, I was afraid to answer Simon's question. I didn't know what it would mean.

"Jenna?" he prompted. "Did you try to use the Board?"

"Yes," I whispered. "The day I found it. I . . . I wanted to talk to my mom."

"Oh, God," Simon said. "That explains the weather."

I looked outside. "What about it?"

"You've awakened the Board, Jenna!" Simon said. "That's . . . why would . . ." His voice trailed off as he looked for and failed to find any words.

"Big deal," I said. "So I played with it for a minute. Now you want me to believe I'm responsible for the weather?"

"Look around you," he said. "This Board is the Board of the Winds, and guarding it is your sacred trust. It has been for generations. But I'm not aware of anyone actually *using* the Board in . . . a very, very long time. That's why the weather has gone crazy. You've awakened it."

I scoffed. "You make it sound like it's alive or something."

Simon's voice turned deadly serious. "In many ways, Jenna, if what I've learned is true, the Board *is* alive."

I felt something snap inside me at that statement. "Are you listening to yourself right now?" I yelled. "Do you hear how crazy you sound? I can't take another second of this . . . this . . . madness! I don't believe in magic, and I don't want to be the Keeper and I don't want the Board!" Something in me twisted again, and I kept a grimace off my face with an effort, turning it into a frown instead.

"Jenna, you're acting like a child," Simon said. "You have responsibilities now that you cannot ignore."

"Fine! I'm acting like a child. I can do that if I want."

Simon took my hand, trying to calm me, and I snatched it away.

"And another thing," I shouted. "Stop touching me! I don't like how you make me feel . . . like I'm . . . like I've stuck my finger in an electrical socket." I gasped for air, realizing what I'd just said, and knowing that I couldn't take the words back now.

The car was silent for a long minute, the only sounds were the winds in the trees, the river, the heater fans, and my panicked breathing.

Finally, Simon said, "What do you mean by that?"

Ashamed by my outburst, I was glad that it was so dark in the car. "I don't know."

"Jenna, I . . ."

I cut him off. "Look, Simon, you show up here out of the blue and expect me to just believe in things that I've spent my whole life believing weren't real. I've never been threatened before, and in the last few days, my house has been broken into, I've been spied on, harassed over the phone, accosted at a church, mugged, kidnapped, and dumped in a river to drown. This is not the kind of life I want."

Simon nodded. "I understand," he said. "I really do. All of this must be very difficult for you to believe. I expected you to know more."

"That's not the half of it," I said. "I just want my old life back."

I heard myself saying it again, and wished there were a better way to express it. Maybe it wasn't that I wanted my old life back—bringing back the dead wasn't really an option—but that I wanted the sudden strangeness in my life to stop.

"Not everyone gets to pick their ideal life," Simon said. "Some people have a destiny, a fate, and that can be both a blessing and a curse."

"Well then, mine's a curse," I said. "I want to go home now."

"I think we should talk about this some more," he said. "If we're going to retrieve the Board, we have much to discuss."

"You don't get it, do you?" I snapped. "We aren't going to retrieve the Board. I do not, repeat *do not,* want it."

Simon pointed outside to the wind-tossed trees. "The Board is yours, Jenna, whether you want it or not."

I crossed my arms. "No, it's not. I don't have to take it, do I?"

A part of me, though, wanted the Board and what it might represent—power and freedom.

"It's a part of you now," he said. "That's why you didn't drown. The Board protects the Keeper . . . just as it endangers the Keeper. I don't know what it means that you've used it, but we have to get it back before the weather gets really out of hand. It could destroy the whole town."

"Don't exaggerate," I said. "That's not a very charming trait."

"What makes you think I'm exaggerating?" he asked. "The Board is dangerous, Jenna, if it's not kept under very tight control. That's why it has a Keeper."

"Are you going to take me home or not?"

"Not until you face up to your responsibilities, no," Simon said.

"Fine, then," I said, opening the door. "I'll walk!"

"You'll freeze to death in those wet clothes," he warned.

I ignored him.

"You can't run away from your responsibilities forever!"

"No?" I asked. "Watch me!" I turned my back on him and walked into the darkness.

My grandfather used to tell me that I'd always hated being wrong. Even as a young child. Walking down the road, I realized something else I hated being: wrong *and* soaking wet. My cell phone was in my backpack along with the Board and I had no real sense of how far I was from town. I stomped along, wondering if Simon was actually going to let me walk.

When I heard the car approaching slowly behind me, I sighed in relief. Like almost every man on the planet, Simon had a hero complex: he had to save the maiden in distress.

I slowed and turned around, but the relief I felt faded almost as quickly as it had surfaced. The vehicle wasn't the sedan Simon had been driving, but a little two-door gas saver that looked familiar.

Could it be the men who'd been chasing me? Or even the one who'd broken into my house?

The driver pulled up next to me, stopped, and rolled the window down.

"Jenna? What on earth are you doing out here?"

I peered inside to see Kristen sitting behind the wheel.

"Kristen!" I said, opening the passenger door. "Thank goodness." I glanced down the road to see if Simon might be pulling up behind us, and while there was a car in the distance, I couldn't be sure it was him, and I couldn't miss out on the ride. I climbed into the warm car. "I was out walking along the river, collecting my thoughts."

"I was hoping to do a little star-gazing, myself," she said, pointing into the backseat where a large telescope rested. "But the clouds never really broke, and this wind is enough to drive anyone indoors." She looked at me critically. "You know, I'll admit that my sense of fashion is a little warped, but what happened to you?"

Thinking fast, I muttered, "Fell in the river."

"You're kidding!" she said. "That happened to me just last year. Oh, goddess, was that water cold! You're lucky you didn't drown or something." She put the car in gear and started down the road.

"How'd you fall in?" she asked. Thankfully, before I had to come up with a creative lie, she added, "I was out here walking along the river—it was about this time of year, too—and thinking about this and that and some of the old stories and myths about water sprites and elementals. Anyway, I wasn't looking where I was going and tripped on a rock, slid down the bank and fell right into the river."

I nodded sympathetically, not having any trouble at all imagining this happening to Kristen. "How'd you get out?" I asked.

She smiled shyly, then whispered. "Tom. Tom saved me."

"You're joking," I said. "He never mentioned that to me— and Tom tells me everything."

"Well, he probably tells you almost everything," Kristen said. "He doesn't like to talk about it."

"Why?" I asked, remembering my thoughts about men wanting to be heroes.

She giggled. "He saw me go in—the water was really deep and running pretty fast—and he ran down to the water to get me. For some reason, he about tore off all his clothes before jumping in." She paused, laughing harder. "So, ummm . . . well, he forgot something."

Infected by her laugh, I chuckled, too. "What?" I asked.

"He was going commando that day," she said, bursting into hysterics.

"Commando?" I asked, not following her.

She rolled her eyes. "No underwear!"

"Oh my God!" I said. We both started laughing hysterically. "He didn't have on . . ."

"Not a stitch . . ." she said, trying to catch her breath.

"So he's running down the river bank and . . ."

"You got it," Kristen crowed. "Just flapping in the breeze!"

"What did you do?" I asked, trying to get myself under control.

"I *looked,* silly," she said. "But I was laughing so hard, even while being half-drowned, that I didn't get to see much." She waggled her eyebrows suggestively. "I fixed that later."

I sighed. "I bet you did."

"What did Tom do?" I asked. "Did he say anything?"

This got her to laughing again. "He didn't know," she said.

"He didn't know what?"

"He didn't even notice until after he'd saved me!" she cried. "We were standing on the riverbank—me in my soaked clothes and coughing and spitting up mud—and Tom's just standing there, patting me on the back and asking if I'm okay."

"No!" I said. "Not a chance."

"I swear," she said. "I was laughing so hard I couldn't tell him. Finally, I just started pointing and that's when he looked down and realized he was naked!"

We laughed all the way into town, both of us with tears running down our faces. It was easy to imagine why Kristen had fallen for him, and vice versa, as that was the first time they met. It felt good to be laughing so openly, and with a friend, for the first time in days. I couldn't tell Kristen everything, but for a few minutes, it was nice to just be nineteen again.

"So," she asked as we pulled up to a stoplight. "Where am I taking you?"

"The home of our hero," I said. "He told you I had a break-in, didn't he?"

Kristen nodded, her face turning serious. "Yeah, he mentioned it."

"Kristen, is it okay that I'm staying there for a couple of days? I don't want you to think . . ." I shrugged. "You know."

She smiled. "I know," she said. "But you and Tom are best friends, and I know your interest in him is strictly platonic."

"Very much so," I said, wanting to reassure her. "He's wonderful, but not really my type."

"That's because you haven't seen him run naked down a river bank," she said. "Hi-ho, Silver, away!"

That set us both off again and we laughed all the way to Tom's house. Kristen and I had never been especially close, but it felt like we were becoming good friends. I wasn't the kind of person to make friends easily, and it had been a long time since I'd felt this close to another woman. Still, given the strange circumstances of my life over the last few days, I also couldn't risk trusting Kristen too soon.

As we pulled up to Tom's building, she found a spot on the street and parked. "Here you go," she said. "The castle of our hero."

I smiled. "Thanks for the lift."

"No problem," Kristen said. She reached out and grasped my arm. "Jenna, I know you and Tom both think I'm a ditz—"

I tried to interrupt her, but she continued on. "No, I know you both do. And in a lot of ways, I am." She grinned. "I don't know what all is going on in your life right now, Jenna, but it smacks of strangeness, and regardless of anything else you might think, that is my one area of expertise. So . . . if you ever need a friend . . ."

"Thanks, Kristen," I said. "I'm not quite ready to . . . tell everything yet, but when I am, you'll be the second person I talk to." I patted her hand. "And I don't think you're a ditz—you just believe in . . . well . . . everything."

"Saves time," she said. "Sooner or later, I'll be right on the money."

I sighed. "You're more right than you know, Kristen." I climbed out of the car, then leaned down and offered a wave. "Thanks again."

"No problem, Jenna. Give a yell if you need anything, okay?"

"I will," I said. "Drive safe."

"Always do," she said. She put the car in gear and drove away. I watched until she turned the corner.

The winds continued howling through the trees and I trudged across the street in my wet socks. I thought about Simon and why he hadn't driven after me. Why I felt the way I did whenever I was around him.

My grandfather used to tell me that one day I would meet someone—the perfect someone for me—and it would feel like I'd been hit by a bolt of lightning. Is that what I was feeling whenever I heard Simon's voice, felt his hand or even saw him?

I started up the steps to Tom's apartment, shaking my head. It couldn't be that . . . it had to be that he was kind of a threat. It was only when he showed up that my life had gotten so complicated and dangerous.

That had to be it, I reassured myself.

I knocked on the door to Tom's apartment, and I heard him unlock the door. He opened it, saw me, and a look of alarm crossed his features. "Jenna! Are you all right?" He ushered me inside, closing the door behind us and locking it.

I went into the living room and tried to figure out where to sit. My clothes were still pretty wet.

I stared blindly around the room, then sighed, but before I could speak, Tom peeled off Simon's coat and tossed it in a corner. Speaking quietly, he took my hand and said, "Come on, Jenna. You need a hot bath and some rest."

I followed him into the bathroom, and he got the water started and then turned back to me. "Take as long as you like, okay? We can talk later."

Relieved not to have to explain everything right away, I nodded my thanks.

"I'm going to run out and get us something to eat. Make yourself comfortable and get out of those wet clothes. You can borrow some of my sweats when you're done—they're in the dresser."

"Thanks, Tom," I said, eyeing the warm water in the tub with something like passion. "Thanks for everything."

"That's what friends are for," he said. "See you in a bit."

After he left, I locked myself in the bathroom and soaked in hot water up to my chin. It felt heavenly to be warm and to not be answering questions. To know I was safe and that Tom would take care of me, at least for tonight.

And when I started to cry, I was glad no one could hear me.

10

"My Lord, we haven't been able to locate her yet.
Even in this small town, she seems to have gone to
ground."

"Then flush her out."

By the time Tom got back with the food and coffee, I'd
managed to pull myself together, wash my hair and get
out of the tub. I even found his sweat suit, which hung on
me like a tent and would have provided modesty for a girl
four times my size. But I was warm, safe and comfortable,
and that was a blessed relief compared to the rest of the day
I'd just had.

Tom let me eat in peace, and didn't pester me with questions, though I knew he must have been itching with curios-

ity. It couldn't be every day that someone showed up at his door half-drowned and mostly frozen. I finished my burger and fries, each bite a little bit of manna to my empty belly, then leaned back and sipped my coffee—a quadruple-shot Grande mocha that would have had most people buzzing around like a housefly all night long. In my case, it just about took the edge off.

Finally, Tom cleared his throat. "Feeling better?" he asked.

I nodded. "Yes, thanks," I said, noting that my voice was a little hoarse. I'd probably have a wicked cold tomorrow. "I . . . thanks for your help."

"I'm your friend, Jenna," he said simply.

"I know," I replied. "And that's why I'm going to tell you everything. I need a friend right now, Tom, to help me figure some of this stuff out."

"Okay," he said, settling back into his chair. "Lay it on me."

"One thing," I said. "You have to promise to keep all this a secret—even from Kristen—unless I say it's okay. When you hear what I have to tell you, you'll probably want to have me locked up—and I'm not sure I would disagree with you."

"Hmmm," Tom said. "How about a compromise?"

"What?"

"I won't tell anyone about it *unless* I think you're in serious danger," he said. "I won't be responsible for you getting hurt." He shrugged. "Besides, Jenna, I think you are in danger—maybe a lot, I don't know for sure. But I won't spill your secret unless I have no other choice."

"My hero," I said, thinking of my conversation with Kristen. It would have been so easy to get sidetracked and start teasing Tom about it, but I sensed that Kristen had told me the story in confidence, even if she hadn't said so. "Fair enough," I said, trying not to smirk at the imagined picture of Tom in the buff and dripping wet.

"So tell me everything," Tom said.

And I did. I told him about seeing the strange man at my grandfather's funeral and finding the Board in the attic. The mysterious voice that kept whispering the name Shalizander. The intruder breaking into my house. Simon. Professor Martin's betrayal and Burke and Tanner kidnapping me and trying to kill me. I even told him about my strange ability to breathe underwater.

Tom sat quietly throughout the whole story, and when I finished, he didn't say anything for a long time. Finally, he stirred and said, "That's quite a story, Jenna."

Crestfallen, I said, "You don't believe me, do you?"

He held up his hands. "I'm not saying I do, and I'm not saying I don't. I want to think about it all for a little while. You've got to admit that it's quite a tale."

"If you'd come to me with the same story," I admitted, "I'd probably already be dialing the loony bin. But do you think I'm the kind of person to make something like this up?"

"No, I don't, which is why I'm not jumping to any conclusions at the moment," he said. "But give me the night to think about and I'll get back to you in the morning." He looked at his watch. "Besides, it's late. You're exhausted and need to rest. We'll talk more tomorrow."

I opened my mouth to protest, and Tom shook his head. "Jenna, I need to digest all this, and you need to get some sleep. Take the bedroom and I'll crash on the sofa again."

Seeing that he wasn't going to budge, I agreed. "Thanks," I said, as I stepped by him and kissed him lightly on the cheek. "Thanks for being my friend, for at least listening and giving me a place to stay."

"That's what friends do," Tom said. "Now go get some sleep."

We said our goodnights and as I went into the bedroom, I realized that he'd been right about one thing; I was completely exhausted. I curled up under the blankets and in the seconds before my eyes closed, I thought about Simon holding me close, and how I was sure I would be too tired to dream that night.

The winds surround me, swirling like invisible dervishes. My hair lashes my face, the strands dark red whips wet with rain.

I raise the Board high in my arms. Its voice calls to me, singing a song of Power. The language is melodic and strange, but I can make it out if I concentrate . . . it is calling the wind. Stronger, faster, the winds keep blowing, rushing around me, drowning out everything else. I felt like I could conquer the world with a gesture, level forests with a glance.

Surrounded by the whirling vortex of air, I feel my body rise into the sky, held aloft by the powerful kiss of the invisible element embracing me. My element. Singing. Growing stronger.

I want a storm—a great beast of wind, and I call to the Board. My voice is swept away, but my thought is clear: "Bring me a storm of wind, a stalker cloaked in air!"

The Board answers and I feel the power of it running in my veins. It is intoxicating . . . like a good red wine or the feel of my lover's lips when they brush my neck. The winds howl now, angry, as though they do not wish to answer my call.

But they will . . . and they do.

Soon I am in a funnel of wind, borne up higher and higher—not flying yet not falling—and around me the swirling cones of five . . . ten . . . a dozen tornadoes breach the sky and reach down with dark gray fingers to slam into the ground below.

Debris rises into the air, hurled by the force of my storm. Trees, houses, animals . . . people . . . all are torn to pieces before the might of my creation. I feel so alive, carried into the heart of this wild beast and riding it like a master horseman.

I call out to the Board again and again, and the winds answer, now in vengeful triumph. Growing ever stronger, swirling faster and faster until it seems that the very sky itself is mine to do with as I want.

Far below, I can see a small house. The house I grew up in. The house of darkness where bad things happened and they told me I could not trust the Board, that I must not use it. The house where my real father had left me before coming back and taking me to the island and the Knights and all their questions.

I look down on the house and know that the storm, my storm, is about this house. Is about revenge and making them pay for not letting me taste this glorious sensation. I am the mistress of the winds . . . the Keeper . . . the Keeper of the Board . . .

And the command of this element is mine. It is the first thing I have ever controlled in my life and I will destroy those who have held me down, held me back, kept me from my trust. I feel the winds around me . . . waiting for my command . . .

I see my stepfather come outside, fear lighting his features. He is superstitious and to him it must appear that I have become a witch. I point to him, to the house, to the empty fields beyond, to the river and scream out my will . . . "Destroy it all!"

The tornadoes descend and the last I see of him is his arms pumping as he tries to run away . . . but there will be no escape . . . no escape for any of them . . .

I woke to the sounds of the television and Tom tapping on the bedroom door. His voice was quiet but firm. "Jenna, you've got to wake up now. I think it's important."

For a moment, I simply lay there, keeping my eyes closed. The dream—vision?—had been amazingly real. Who was the woman I had been? Some distant ancestor who also held the Board and the role of Keeper? Did consciously using the Board always feel so intense, so good?

Tom knocked again, and I opened my eyes. "I'm awake," I called. "What is it?"

"I think you need to get up," he said, his voice muted behind the door. "Something's happened."

I climbed out of bed and opened the door. "What is it?" I asked.

Looking beyond me, Tom gasped. "What happened in here?"

I turned around and realized that the room was in shambles. The window blinds had been torn down, the dresser was overturned and all of Tom's clothing and shoes were scattered across the room. "I don't . . ." Stunned, I couldn't find the words.

"It looks like . . ." Tom started, then stopped. "You need to see this," he finished. He guided me into the living room where the television was on.

A haggard newscaster was giving the morning report. Behind him, scenes of devastation were shown over and over again. "Last night's bizarre series of tornadoes are still puzzling meteorologists across the state and the nation," he said. "The phenomenon was incredibly localized, and quite possibly the worst storms to hit our area in over a century." A scene of the local shopping mall—ravaged and destroyed—

appeared on the screen. "The destruction on the outskirts of Miller's Crossing and a number of suburbs is almost total. Meteorologists tracked almost a dozen tornadoes that touched down as they spread across the county and unleashed damaging winds with horrific force."

"Oh, my God," I whispered. Did the Board do that? Did *I* do that?

The newscaster continued. "The tornadoes came literally out of nowhere, without any indication that they were going to touch down. According to emergency rescue workers, the death toll currently stands at twenty-three, but is expected to go higher, possibly much higher, as more workers are able to get to homes and commercial buildings. The local hospital, St. Mary's, has been overwhelmed with injured residents, and no estimate has yet been given for those people—or for total property damage caused by the storms. The governor is expected to declare the area a disaster—"

Tom reached out and shut off the television. "Jenna," he said quietly, "is there anything you're not telling me?"

I shook my head wildly. "No, of course not!" I said. "I told you everything I know."

"Then how did my room get destroyed?" he asked.

"Well . . . ummm . . . if I did it, how come you didn't hear it?" I challenged.

"How come *you* didn't hear it?" he snapped back. "I was gone. After you fell asleep last night, I went over to Kristen's. Both of us spent the night huddled in her basement. I only just now got here."

"I don't know why I didn't hear it!"

"Well, you're lucky the whole building didn't come down around your ears!" Tom shouted.

"Don't yell at me!"

In two strides, Tom closed the distance between us and took me in his arms, wrapping me in a strong hug. "Oh, God, Jenna," he whispered. "I'm sorry. I've spent half the night worried sick about you, but I couldn't leave Kristen. I tried to call, but the lines were down, and my cell wasn't working either."

Feeling my anger drain out of me, I relaxed against him. "It's okay. I'm sorry about your room."

"To hell with the room," he said. "I'm just glad you're safe."

"Am I?" I asked. "I'm beginning to wonder."

"I guess I can't blame you for that," Tom admitted. "But we'll figure out what's going on eventually."

"I hope so," I said, wondering if he was trying to comfort himself or me. "So now what?"

Tom reluctantly let me out of his arms, and then pointed to the kitchen. "Breakfast," he said.

"Breakfast?"

He nodded. "Can't fight a war on an empty stomach," he said.

"Is that what we're doing?" I asked. "Fighting a war?"

"I don't know for sure," he said. "But I'm beginning to think so."

"Then breakfast sounds wonderful." I followed him into

the kitchen, where we made scrambled eggs, bacon, toast and coffee.

It was quiet and pleasant, and I did my best to not think about the people on the outskirts of town who had died in the storm last night. It was hard to reconcile that with the feelings of awe and power from my dream the night before. How could they be connected? What was the Board really?

After we finished eating, Tom put our dishes in the sink to soak, and then sat down. "Better?" he asked.

I smiled. "As good as I'm likely to get anyway." I sipped my coffee. "Have you decided yet?"

"What's that?" he asked.

"If you believe me?"

"To be honest, I don't want to believe you, Jenna," he said. "But I do. You aren't the lying kind, and there's nothing else to explain what's going on. What do they call it when the most simple explanation is the best one?"

I thought about it for a moment, then snapped my fingers. "Occam's Razor," I said. "Essentially, when multiple explanations for a phenomenon are possible, the simplest one is usually correct." Then I shook my head. "Nothing very simple about this."

"No," he admitted, "but there are also far too many coincidences for them to *not* be connected. You find a strange board called the Board of Winds, then you start having weird dreams and visions, then strange people show up and the weather goes crazy, and so on. It's all too close together. It must be connected somehow."

"So, what do I do now?"

"Do you want it back? The Board, I mean," he said.

I thought about it. I would like to say no, to tell him the same thing I'd told Simon the night before, but the truth was . . . "Yes," I said simply. "More than anything I've ever wanted. It's a part of me, I guess. I'm not sure how or why, but there it is."

Tom nodded. "That's what I thought. So we have to figure out how to get it back from Burke."

"If he still has it and hasn't sold it already," I said. "Remember, he thinks I'm dead."

Tom was about to reply when someone knocked on his door. Three solid raps. "Hold that thought," he said. "I'll be right back."

He got up and went into the living room, and I heard him pause briefly. He must have been looking out the peephole to see who it was. Almost a full minute passed and whoever had knocked got impatient and tried again. Tom grumbled something under his breath and then I heard him unlock the door.

"I suppose you better come in," he said.

"Thank you," I heard a familiar voice reply.

Sagging, I waited for what I knew was coming. Tom entered the kitchen with his guest right behind.

We stared at each other, not saying anything for several heartbeats and then Tom broke the silence. "You must be Simon," he said.

"Yes, I am," Simon said. He extended a hand. "Simon Monk."

"A cruel name," Tom said, shaking his hand. "I'm Tom." He arched an eyebrow at Simon. "How'd you get stuck with that particular name combination?"

"I was abandoned," Simon replied, once more touching the coin around his neck, "and grew up in a Catholic orphanage. They didn't know my real name, so they gave me one."

I resolved to ask him more about his strange piece of jewelry one day, but just then wasn't the time.

"An interesting choice," Tom said. "No doubt you know the history of that name?"

"Indeed," Simon said. "He was a revolutionary of sorts, longing for faith and yet fascinated by science."

"A-hem!" I said. "Hello?"

"Sorry," they both said at once.

"Good morning, Jenna," Simon said. "Rough night?"

"You could say that," I said. "But, please, don't let me interrupt this fascinating discussion on the history of the name Simon. My problems can wait."

"Jenna, there's no need to be rude," Tom said.

"What? What?" I stammered. "No need to be rude? He left me to almost freeze to death in the river! He let me walk home in the rain! All of this may be his fault, for all I know. And you're worried about my manners?"

Tom grinned. "No, I'm not worried about your manners, but I think we may need his help."

"Why?" I asked.

"Think about it," he said. "So far, Simon is the only person—

other than me—that's even tried to help you. He may have the social graces of a yak, but he's still trying to help."

"Thanks," Simon said. "I think."

"That doesn't explain why you almost let Jenna die," Tom said. "Maybe that's a good place to start."

"*I* think that's a great idea," I said. "Why did you almost let me die?"

"I didn't," Simon said, holding up his hands. "Not exactly."

"What part of letting me sink to the bottom of the river and then almost freeze to death was the 'not exactly' part?" I asked.

"The part where I don't know how to swim," Simon said.

The room went utterly silent. "Ummm . . ." I said. "You don't?"

"Not a stroke," he said.

"Well why didn't you say that last night!"

"I didn't get a chance," Simon said. "You took off before I could tell you much of anything, if you'll recall."

"And then you let me go off down the road by myself!" I shouted. "I could have frozen to death."

"That girl picked you up," Simon said. "I wasn't that far behind her, and when I saw you get in the car, I followed until you got here and went inside."

"Oh, you two were absolutely *made* for each other," Tom said, laughing. "Can't you tell?"

"NO!" we both said together.

Tom continued laughing, leaving us glaring at each other. After we had all calmed down, I said, "Okay, Simon, you've got my attention and if Tom says I should hear you out, I will. If I don't figure out what's going on soon, I'm going to have myself committed." I was trying to make a joke out of it, but from the looks on Simon's and Tom's faces, it fell flat.

"It will be worse than that," Simon said, his tone deep and serious. "If I can't get you to accept what's going on, the Board will destroy Miller's Crossing and many more people will die. Worse still, you may be killed yourself. There are forces involved in this that you simply don't understand yet."

All of us were silent as Simon's words sank in. I leaned back in my chair and sipped my coffee, wrapping my hands around the warm mug to keep them from trembling.

"All right, Simon," I said. "Sit down and help me understand what I need to know."

Simon sat down and Tom followed suit. After everyone was comfortable, Simon continued, "I don't know everything about the Boards, but I've been able to pick up quite a bit by doing a lot of research. The records in the Vatican go back for thousands of years, and they also have the largest collection of occult knowledge in the world."

"Why?" I asked. "It doesn't make sense."

"Sure it does," Tom said. "Know your enemy, right?"

"That's exactly right," Simon replied. "From its earliest days, the Church has kept records of occult movements and artifacts, gathering them for safekeeping whenever possible, destroying them when it wasn't."

"And that's what you do for them?" I asked.

Simon shrugged. "Sort of," he said. "But let's not get off track. We need to start with the most important thing for you to know."

"What's that?" I asked, leaning forward.

"Those storms last night?" Simon said.

"Yes?"

"You created them, Jenna," he said softly. "And if you don't get control of the Board soon, even more people will die."

"The good news is that we've located the girl, my Lord. The bad news is that she's with Simon. And they're talking."

"More Vatican nonsense, no doubt. The more time she spends away from the Board, the more she'll need it. We'll let her dangle for a bit, then make the young lady an offer she won't dare refuse."

"My Lord?"

"Go pick up our bait."

I just sat there for a moment, struggling to comprehend Simon's words. How could I have been responsible for last night's destruction? "What do you mean, 'more people will die'?"

"Just what I said, Jenna," Simon said. "When you used the Board, you awakened its powers. That's why the winds have been so out of control in this area."

"So why can't she just . . . I don't know . . . tell it to stop?" Tom asked.

"Let me guess, I need the Board to do that, I think," I said. "Right?"

Simon nodded. "I believe so, yes."

"Hold on a minute," I said. "Can we please just start at the beginning? You're jumping around too much."

"Sorry," Simon said, sighing. "I've been researching this subject for years, and I forget that you haven't been told much."

"I haven't been told *anything*!" I said.

"Not for my lack of trying, however."

At the look on my face, he held up his hand. "But fair enough, I suppose." He took another sip of coffee and grimaced. "Not as good as yours," he said.

Tom and I grinned at each other. Making the best coffee was a long-running dispute between us. "You win," he said.

"I know."

We both chuckled, enjoying the shared moment of normality before plunging back into chaos. "So let's have it, Simon," Tom said.

He nodded. "We are short on time, but I'll give you the condensed version of what I've learned, okay?"

"Okay," I said.

"The Boards are magical artifacts," he began, but before he could finish his sentence Tom interrupted.

"Whoa!" he said. "Stop right there. You said 'boards'—plural. There's more than one of these things?"

"Yes," Simon said. "Originally, there were thirteen Boards, though there were only nine creators. All master sorcerers of some kind. Some of the texts mention a 'master Board,' so my surmise is that there are at least nine Boards—three sets of three each—and each set can be somehow combined into a fourth, separate board."

"And *all* of these are still around?" I asked.

"I don't know for sure," Simon said. "It's possible, maybe even probable. The one thing I'm fairly certain of from all my research is that they can't be destroyed by any conventional means."

Tom started to ask another question, but Simon stopped him with a look. "Are you going to let me tell you what I know or keep asking me questions all morning?"

"Probably both," Tom admitted, "but I'll let you talk first."

"Thank you," Simon said.

I couldn't tell if he was being serious or sarcastic.

"Before you go on, *I* have a question," I said.

"What's that?" he asked.

"So if there are that many Boards, how many—what did you call me—Keepers are there?"

Simon's shoulders sagged. "That was something I was hoping you wouldn't ask," he said.

"Why?"

"Because unless I'm mistaken there's only ever been one."

"For *all* of them?!" I asked, trying not to shout and failing miserably.

"It's complicated," Simon said. "If you both will please let me continue?"

Tom and I nodded.

"Good," he said. "Either way, a certain number of the Boards were originally created. How many of them still exist is uncertain, but as I said, it's very likely that all of them do. Where the others are, I cannot say for sure, though there are some clues about their last known locations around."

"If my Board is the Board of the Winds, what are the others?" I asked.

"The first set of Boards are called the Boards of the Elements—I have read that there is one Board for each of the elements—Air, Water, Fire, and Earth, though which is the master Board, I don't know for sure."

"And the others?" Tom asked.

Simon shrugged. "The information is a bit—sketchier on the others. I've only found scattered fragments about the rest of them. According to one of the texts—Sumerian, as I recall, the powers of the Boards stack, going higher from control of the basic elements to animals to . . . humanity itself."

I can't believe I'm buying this, but what choice do I have? If this is true, what horrific things those sorcerers made. I shuddered.

"From what I've been able to find out, Jenna," Simon continued, "the line of Solitaire women goes back in a single, straight line for generations. I don't know for sure how many, but your lineage goes back to at least the Crusades, maybe longer. The Board of the Winds has been passed down from mother to daughter until you came along. Since your mother and your grandmother died, you were never told about your special legacy."

"Good for me," I said.

"No, not good," he replied. "Had your mother or grandmother lived, they could have told you that you should *never* attempt to use the Board. It's too late now, however. What's done is done. If my information is accurate, the next Board will soon begin responding to the magical call of the Board of the Winds."

"You make them sound like they're alive," Tom said. "How can that be? They're just made of wood."

"Not just wood," I said, startling everyone, including myself. "That Board—there's something else about it—like something trapped inside it. I can't explain it, but I felt it when I tried to use it that night." I thought of the voice that whispered in my mind whenever I had held it or when I'd been in danger. "It's alive."

"That sounds about right—each Keeper is attuned to the Boards themselves," Simon said. "I don't understand it myself, but I've been told that the Boards are . . . aware in some strange way and that they call to each other in turn. They want to be found and used."

"Why?" I asked. "And who told you?"

"That's a long bit of history," Simon said. "To summarize, there once lived a man named Jacques de Molay, a Templar Knight whose illegitimate daughter was a Solitaire. He tried to protect her, and was executed for demon worship during the Crusades. She disappeared shortly thereafter, and the records at the time made it sound like she drowned." He smiled briefly at me. "As you now know, that's not possible for someone who possesses the Board."

"The Templar Knights?" Tom said. "We read something about them online."

"Yes," Simon said. "After that, they split into at least two factions, maybe more. At least one of them still exists today in the form of a secret society that has dedicated itself to the study and recovery of magical artifacts like the Boards. Much of the information I've discovered has come from them." He paused and seemed about to say more, but then stopped.

"And what is the Keeper's role?" Tom asked.

"Historically, it's been to protect the Board of the Winds. The specifics of why are lost to history, perhaps to ensure that the rest of the Boards aren't located or used. Given last night's storms, I'm beginning to see why. Now, though, with the Board awakened—"

"What?" I asked.

"There is a legend, an ancient prophecy really, that the last Keeper would be the one to master all of the Boards. All thirteen of them. And that she would somehow protect the world from some great catastrophe," Simon said. "What that great catastrophe would be, however, is unclear."

"What's to say that Jenna is the last Keeper?" Tom asked. "Some day, she could have a daughter and the cycle could go on for who knows how long."

I dropped my gaze to the tabletop and shook my head. "I'm the last," I said quietly. "I know that much anyway."

Simon's eyes widened. "How?"

"I . . . I can't have children," I said. "Not ever."

"What? Why?" Tom said.

"A birth defect," I said, shrugging.

"Good Lord," Simon said. "So Armand's suspicions were correct."

"Who is Armand?" I asked.

"Armand Legard. He leads the secret sect of the Templar Knights," Simon explained. "It was his information that lead me here and to you. He thought you might be the last."

"How did he find me?" I asked.

"He didn't say," Simon admitted. "But I'm glad he did. If he hadn't . . . who knows what might have happened."

"My life would have gone on normally?" I guessed. "College, a career, maybe a husband?"

"Your sarcasm is amusing," Simon said. "But not very helpful. You have a decision to make, Jenna."

"What's that?" Tom asked. "She gets a choice?"

"Sure she does," Simon said. "Free will is a covenant from God. We all get to choose."

"So what's mine?" I asked, wanting to cut to the chase.

"You can accept your destiny as the Keeper of the Boards, get the Board of the Winds back, and go after the others . . . or not, and pray that someone or something doesn't get the Boards and use them for evil first. That the prophecy is wrong and there is no great catastrophe about to befall the Earth. That you are not the last Keeper."

"That's a lousy choice," Tom complained.

"That's life," Simon countered without looking at him. "Most choices like this are . . . lousy." He regarded me intently. "What do you say, Jenna? Will you accept your role as the Keeper, your destiny? Or will you just walk away from it all and leave the world to the chaos you created by accident?"

The kitchen was silent for long minutes as I sat quietly and thought about everything that had happened over the last few days. I thought about my grandfather and the family I had never known and never would. I thought about my visions and dreams. About those dead people killed by the tornadoes conjured somehow by the Board—and perhaps, even conjured somehow by me. I thought about my name and how no one had even known the history of it or where it had come from.

Simon and Tom were both right—either decision was lousy, but when it came down to it, I really had no choice. My mother had been a Keeper. My grandmother. And my grandfather had raised me to try to do the right thing. And at least one thing Simon had said was true—there were people out there that would do anything to possess the Board, even kill for it. If they were willing to do that, what might they do when they got the Board and tried to use it themselves? If a dream of mine could cause such destruction, what could someone who knew what they were doing accomplish?

I looked at the two men in the kitchen—one of whom had been my best friend for years, and the other that made me feel . . . dangerously alive, and nodded.

"The Board," I said to Simon, "was created by a woman named Shalizander. My ultimate grandmother."

Simon's eyes widened. "How do you know that?"

"I dreamed of her," I said. "A true dream. I *was* her."

Simon's eyes lit up at this new knowledge, and he asked, "When? When were the Boards made and where?"

I thought back to the vision, comparing it to my knowledge of history.

"The Boards were made in the Tower of Babylon," I said, remembering how it soared up into the sky. "It's the only place I can think of in antiquity that would have looked even remotely like that."

"Babylon," Simon said, his voice reverent. "Like the coin on my necklace. . . . When?"

"I don't know," I said. "But I do know one thing for sure."

"What's that?" Tom asked.

"I am the last Keeper," I said. "And I have to get my Board back. The rest of it can wait for now."

Simon smiled at me, and for the first time, I saw past the darkness in his eyes to the kindness beneath. I felt the pull of our earlier connection, and a soft floating feeling in the pit of my stomach. How could a man who infuriated me so much also be so attractive to me?

"Then we've got to make a plan," Tom said. "And a good one."

* * *

Standing a block down from Burke's shop, Simon looked at Tom and me again and said, "You both know what to do, right?"

"We've got it," I said. "Let's get this over with. I want it back."

Simon nodded and started up the walk, Tom and I two steps behind. A phone call to make an appointment earlier ensured that the entrance would be open. Simon opened the door and strolled in, leaving it hanging open long enough for Tom and me to slip inside and duck into the shadowy darkness of the rows of shelves. I heard Simon lock it behind us and then he continued deeper into the shop.

Tom and I made our way through the stacks, letting Simon reach the back of the shop well ahead of us. I heard Burke's voice rise in greeting.

"Good afternoon, Mr. Monk," he said.

Like nothing had happened. Like he hadn't tried to kill someone yesterday. I gritted my teeth at his nonchalance. If I'd had the Board right now—

"Good afternoon," Simon said. "Do you have the item?"

Tom and I crept closer and peeked around the corner of a shelf. Tanner was nowhere in sight, but Burke was seated behind the counter, casually talking to Simon.

"We can discuss it," Burke said. "It's quite valuable, you know."

"Oh yes," Simon said. "I'm well aware of its value. That's why I called."

"I'm curious though," Burke said. "I only acquired the item yesterday. How did you come to know I had it?"

"A friend of mine, Professor Martin over at the college, mentioned it," Simon lied smoothly.

For a priest, I thought, *the man lies like a pro.*

"I see," Burke said. "I'll have to thank him the next time we talk." His tone made clear that thanks were the last thing he had in mind. "I have to warn you, however, that there is another party who has already expressed interest in the item. I don't want to start a bidding war, but this is a business, after all."

"I understand," Simon said. "May I ask what the current offer is? I'm willing to pay handsomely for it."

"The current offer stands at one million dollars," Burke said. "Can you beat that?"

Simon nodded. "I think so," he said. "How about avoiding spending the rest of your life in prison?"

Burke's face tightened. "What are you talking about?" he asked.

Simon looked over his shoulder. "Come on out," he called.

Tom and I stepped out around the shelf, and Burke's face whitened. "You . . ." he started, stammering. "You're dead!" he said.

"I'm resilient," I replied. "Where's my Board? Give it back and I won't press charges."

"I can't!" Burke said.

Simon's blue eyes went flat. "Why?"

"It's gone!" Burke said. "The buyer already took it."

"How much was my stolen property worth?" I asked. "Obviously more than my life."

"He offered a million for the Board *and* you," he cried. "But I panicked. I deal in items, not people. I couldn't do it, but I couldn't risk letting you go either!" He gestured at a small suitcase. "He only paid half, five hundred thousand, for the Board itself."

"You're a coward and a thief," Simon said. "Special punishments await those guilty of such sins in the next world."

Trying to calm himself, Burke muttered, "Don't I know it."

"Who was the buyer?" Tom asked.

"I can't tell you that either," he said. "I'd be ruined as a businessman, and that's only if he didn't kill me for revealing his identity."

Simon calmly stepped around the counter. I couldn't explain it, but he seemed almost . . . charged with energy and very, very dangerous at that moment. "You'll be more ruined in prison," he told Burke, his voice low and ominous. "So start talking now, or we'll call the police and let them sort it out."

"Fine," Burke said, holding up his hands. "There's no need to get the law involved. The buyer's name is Peraud."

"How do we find him?" I asked.

"You don't," Burke said. "He finds you." He pulled a scrap of paper out of his pocket. "Here," he said, thrusting it at Simon. "Call that number and leave a message for him. Peraud will get in touch, or one of his men, more likely."

"You've never seen him?" Tom said. "Ever?"

Burke shook his head. "No, I've only dealt with his lackeys. But they came this morning, paid and took the Board."

Thinking about all that money and what I'd lost, I tried not to seethe. Then it hit me. "Where's Tanner?" I said.

"I don't know," Burke said. "I haven't seen him since last night."

"We know enough," Simon said, "but there's still the matter of payment."

"Payment?" Burke asked. "For what? I gave you the number and I don't have the Board."

Simon took two graceful steps and picked up the suitcase. "I don't think you deserve this, Burke," he said. "You have attempted to profit from *stolen* merchandise and it was Jenna's property. This belongs to her."

My eyes widened. That was a *lot* of money.

"But . . ." Burke said, then his shoulders slumped in defeat. When it came down to it, he was essentially a coward. But I should have realized that on the bridge. "Fine," he snapped. "Take it and go."

"One more thing," Simon said, handing the suitcase to Tom. He stepped forward and before Burke could react, grabbed his shirt collar and yanked him forward. "This," he said. Then he slammed his fist into Burke's jaw. "That's for messing with the Keeper in the first place, you little weasel. If you ever come near her again, I'll make *certain* you pay for it dearly."

Dazed, Burke nodded his head in agreement, his hands held up in a vain effort to ward Simon off.

"Are we ready?" Tom asked, watching Burke with wide eyes as he stumbled back several steps, holding his face.

"Almost," I said. "Burke, there is one last thing I want from you."

"What now?" he pleaded. "You've got my money, the contact, and my jaw will hurt for weeks."

"I just want you to deliver a simple message. Tell Professor Martin that the Keeper has returned and he'd better start running right now if he doesn't want me to catch up with him."

Burke blanched. "You . . . you're the Keeper?" he asked. "Martin never said anything about that!"

"You're an idiot," Simon said. "Why do you think she didn't drown? Some specialist you are." He hefted the suitcase and gestured at Tom and me. "Let's go," he said.

We went out the way we'd come in, but the jubilation I'd felt at getting a good lead on the Board was short-lived. Outside, the winds had started to howl again, and in the distance, huge banks of greenish black clouds boiled up in waves. Another storm was brewing and it looked to be even worse than the last one.

Simon saw it, too. "We've got to hurry," he said. "That storm looks like it could break at any time."

We went and climbed into Simon's sedan. "It won't," I said. "Not until tonight."

"How do you know that?" Tom asked.

I shrugged, not sure myself. "I can feel it," I answered. "The winds aren't ready yet."

"Where to?" Simon asked, getting in the driver's seat.

"Back to my house," I said. "We need to figure out our next move."

"Calling Peraud and getting the Board back," Tom said. "Simple."

Simon pulled out of his parking space and headed in the direction of my house. "Somehow," he said, "I don't have a 'simple' feeling about any of this."

Looking at the storm clouds, I whispered, "Neither do I."

*"She has returned to her house, along with Simon
and another man. Forgive my impertinence, my
Lord, but Simon looks . . . exactly like me."*

*"Ah, you have noticed the familial resemblance?
You and he are more closely intertwined than you
know, and we will discuss that later. For now, be sure
to disguise yourself when dealing with either of
them."*

"What of this other man?"

*"Both Simon and he are of no consequence at the
moment. Extend our offer to her. She won't be able to
resist the call of the Board—and will deliver herself
right into our hands."*

By the time we got to my house, the winds were gusting in
great waves. The trees thrashed and cracked in agony,
their branches bent almost double by the lashing gale, and
what few bits of dead leaves and grass left over from the
winter were tossed into the air to swirl away into the heavy
sky. The air smelled like cold rain, but I knew that it wasn't
going to fall just yet.

Simon brought the suitcase with him, setting it down with

a sigh of relief in the hall closet, and saying, "We'll figure out what to do with that later."

I shrugged. It wasn't like I needed money that badly. "Maybe a charity?" I suggested.

"Maybe," he said noncommittally. "We've got a few other things to worry about right now."

"True," Tom said, tossing his coat onto the hook. "Like something warm to drink?" He looked at me with pure desperation in his eyes and I laughed in spite of the circumstances.

"Yes," I said, sighing and thinking I'd have a soda instead. I liked coffee—*a lot*—but I'd had more in the last few days than I usually had in two weeks. "I'll brew some."

Shrugging out of our coats, we walked into the kitchen, and I started the coffee while Tom and Simon discussed this mysterious Peraud and what to do when we managed to get in touch with him. I watched them out of the corner of my eye, thinking about the odd effect Simon had on me. He was dangerous in some way I couldn't put my finger on, and wicked smart. The first was intriguing, but I could have done without it, the second was definitely interesting, to say the least. And there were still those handsome looks of his; I caught myself almost staring at him more than once. I was attracted to him, but intimidated and repelled all at the same time. I wondered if I would ever get the chance to talk to Kristen about it, then laughed to myself. She'd probably tell me we were lovers in a past life!

I poured coffee for everyone and set the tray down on the

kitchen table, but before I could join in the discussion, the phone rang. I changed direction and answered it. The caller ID display read PRIVATE NUMBER. Probably a telemarketer, I thought. "Hello?"

"Jenna?" a hoarse but familiar voice said. "Jenna, don't do what—"

I heard a muffled curse and what sounded like flesh striking flesh, followed by the rattling of a phone hitting the ground. What the—? "Hello?"

Another person came on the line. "Did you hear that voice? Do you know it?" The sound of this voice was strange, like a cloth was being held over the receiver or maybe the connection was bad. "It's your beloved Father Andrew."

"Yes," I said, my eyes widening as I realized that I did know the first voice. "I heard him."

"Good," the voice said. "We have him. We want to make a trade."

Trying to get Simon's attention, I waved my arm frantically. He saw me and trotted over, leaning his head in close enough to the phone for me to smell the leather and musk scent of his aftershave.

"What . . . what kind of trade?" I asked.

"You and the journal for the priest," the voice said.

"Why?" I asked, guessing that this was Peraud or one of his men. "You already have the Board."

"We need the journal, too," the voice replied. "And what good is the Board without the Keeper?"

"If I refuse?" I asked, hating that I already knew the answer.

"Then Father Andrew finds out if his dogma about the afterlife is right," the voice said. "But don't think it will be fast. It won't. We'll do it slow. Make it last a long time. Make him pray."

I shuddered. The menace in the voice confirmed that he spoke the truth. I didn't want Father Andrew hurt simply because he knew me, because I cared about him. Once again, my choices were limited.

"Well?" the voice asked.

"When and where?" I said.

"Tonight, nine o'clock," he said, giving an address for a warehouse in one of the older parts of town. "And come alone. Leave your boyfriend and the fallen priest at home. We don't need any would-be heroes there, just yourself."

"Fine," I said. "Just don't hurt him."

The person on the other end didn't respond for a second, and then chuckled, sending a chill up my spine. "Oh, we won't," he said. "Much." Then he hung up.

I replaced the phone on the cradle and looked at Simon.

He must have read the intent in my eyes. "Jenna," he said softly. "You can't."

"I have to," I said. "What kind of Keeper would I be if I didn't protect those I care about?"

"Can't what?" Tom asked, crossing the kitchen to where Simon and I faced off.

Simon knew that Tom would be a good ally and immediately enlisted his aid. "Trade herself and the journal for Father Andrew."

"Peraud has Father Andrew?" Tom said.

I nodded. "Yes, and I have to do this."

"Jenna," Simon said. "You can't just meet this man. Whoever he is, he must be powerful to command the kind of money and men he obviously has at his disposal. What guarantee do you have that he won't take you, the Board, the journal and just kill Father Andrew?"

"I don't, Simon. But I know what's right. Father Andrew is practically family to me. I can't let them hurt him if I can at least try to stop it."

"But you have a duty!" Simon said.

"To be the Keeper, you said. That's what I'm doing!"

"To guard the Board, yes, but not to foolishly throw your life away. Without you, there is no Keeper."

"Stop!" Tom shouted, stepping between us. "Stop it now!"

Simon and I both realized that we'd closed the distance between us and were practically nose to nose shouting at each other. Furious, I realized that the man could bring out the worst in me in seconds. Apparently, I seemed to have the same effect on him sometimes.

"What is it, Tom?" I said, backing away from Simon and leaning on the counter.

"She's right, Simon," Tom said. "I don't know much about what a Keeper is or does, but I do know who Jenna is. She could no more leave Father Andrew in trouble than she could fly."

Trying not to think of my visions where I'd held the Board

and been able to levitate into the sky, borne aloft by the winds, I nodded in agreement.

"You *agree* with her?" Simon asked, unbelieving. "I thought you wanted to protect her."

"I do," Tom said. "But I wouldn't try to change who she is and neither should you. Father Andrew is basically the only family she has left."

I looked at Tom in surprise. We had always been close, but I hadn't realized how much he knew about my inner emotions. He'd proven himself a good friend countless times over the years and especially over the last few days, but this was the first time I'd really seen how much he knew about *me*. I didn't think I could honestly say I knew him as well. My grandfather used to say that I was a good fit for my name, that I held myself away from others, but I suddenly realized that the truth was that I didn't look deeply into others . . . perhaps for fear of what I might see.

Simon appeared deep in thought, then shrugged. "I can see I've been out-voted," he finally said. "If that is your choice, Jenna, then I will be as supportive as I can."

I almost fell over in shock and my thoughts immediately wondered what Simon was up to. "And?" I said.

"Nothing," he replied, looking at his watch. "But I do have to go if I'm to help."

"Go?" Tom asked. "Where?"

"I cannot say," Simon said. "But I will be around when the time is right." He looked at me sternly. "A lot of being a

Keeper, I think, is about faith. Even if you don't see me right away, Jenna, have a little faith. I'll be there."

Unsure of quite what to say or do, I nodded. "See you tonight then," I whispered.

"Yes," he said. "Tonight." Then he turned and headed to the front door, pausing only to put on his coat and address Tom. "Watch over her as best you can."

"I will," Tom said. "Just be sure you show up."

Simon didn't reply, but slipped quietly out the door.

"I have to admit it," Tom said. "I don't think I like him much."

I wasn't sure what I felt about Simon, so I said, "I think he's a hard person to like in general." The last thing I wanted to admit was that I wanted to like him any more than I already might.

"So what do we do?"

"The only thing we can," I said. "We have to go to your apartment and I need to read more of the journal before tonight."

"Why?" Tom asked. "Aren't you just going to give it to him?"

I shook my head. "Of course not! I want my Board back and I need to learn how to use it."

Tom smiled. "You're going to fight, aren't you?"

I grinned tightly. "Like the Devil himself," I said. "They need me to use the Board, I'm almost certain of it. And that gives me a weapon against them."

We put on our coats and left, taking my grandfather's car

out of the garage, my mind already focusing on the battle that lay ahead of us.

"Call on me and I will answer with all the manifestations of the winds. From the most gentle of breezes to the most fearsome of gales, I am the element of Air. Air is the giver of life, of breath, and so long as I am yours, you will not lack for my powers."

"Who are you?"

"I am part of the whole, yours to command by will and effort. I am one of nine, of thirteen, of the first set. I was created by Shalizander and by her master, too."

"Part of what whole? The nine? The thirteen?"

"Patience. In time you will know more and I will avail you of my ancient knowledge and powers. Your journey shall be mine and together with my brethren, we will open the way."

"The way to what?"

"To the whole . . ."

I turn my attention from the Board and look outside. The winds that have come since I first touched it are fierce, and the trees nearby groan beneath the strain.

"How do I use you?"

"You must master me with your call and I will answer, or I will master you with mine. In time, I will hear you even from a great distance . . . It matters little. We are one and the same. We share hungers."

"For what?"

"For power. For the violent and tender kiss of the storm."

"What storm?"

"Our storm. The one I called when you were angry before. The one coming even now. Can you not feel it?"

I search with my mind outside and realize that I can feel it. It is a monstrous wall of wind that has gathered debris, hail and rain in equal measures and is bearing down on the castle even now. When it gets there . . .

It will destroy them all!

"No!" I say. "That's not what I want."

"It is what you want. Your mind is very clear to me, you hold no secrets. Use me, Keeper. You no longer need to fear."

I feel the surge of power and know the Board is telling the truth. I have nothing to fear. I am powerful and the lord of the castle will not lay a hand on me ever again . . .

"Jenna, can you hear me?"

I wrest myself back from the vision slowly. I am me again. Jenna Solitaire. And someone more now. The last Keeper of the Boards. I have lost my Board.

"Jenna?"

Tom's voice again, worried.

I opened my eyes. "Yes, Tom," I said quietly. "I'm okay, I think. Just tired and thirsty. My head is killing me."

"That was . . . very weird," he said, offering me a glass of water.

Confused, I said, "Why? What happened?"

He showed me his watch. "You opened the journal and it was like . . . I don't know . . . you just went into a trance of some kind. You've been silent for almost two hours. I didn't think you were in any real danger, but I was starting to get worried." He grinned. "It might have been tough to explain your condition to a paramedic."

Stunned, I said, "But it was only . . . it didn't seem like that long. A few seconds maybe, or a minute at the most."

"If you hadn't still been breathing, I'd have called an ambulance. It was almost like you weren't here at all."

"I wasn't," I said, thinking about the last time I'd opened the book. "When I read the journal, I don't really read. I *become* whoever wrote the entry in my mind, seeing what they saw when they lived it."

"That's . . . that's horrible," Tom said. "What kind of magic is that?"

I thought about my visions and, dismissing the aftereffects, said, "Good magic. I can learn more by experiencing something than just reading about it."

"Strange," he said. "So what did you learn?"

"I'm not sure yet," I admitted. "It's not like this book is the instruction manual of the Boards, you know. I see parts, often not everything—it's hard to put it into context sometimes. I need to think about it some more."

Tom looked pointedly at his watch again. "Yeah, that

would probably be wise, but I don't think we have a lot of time left, you know."

"I know," I said. "But it will come to me, I hope."

"For all our sakes, I hope so, too," he said. "Are you ready to go?"

"We've got a little while before we have to be there," I said. "What's your rush? You're in a hurry to meet the bad guy?"

"No," Tom said. "But I do want one last latte before I die, if it's okay with you." He grinned, proving that his sense of humor was still working at least.

"That's a pretty good idea," I replied. "I could use a quad-shot myself."

"I don't know how you do that," he said, putting on his jacket and handing mine to me. "I'd be awake and trembling in a corner for hours."

"It doesn't seem to affect me that way," I said. "Besides, you might try it yourself now."

"Why?"

"It's not going to be a good night to fall asleep early."

"You've got a point there," he said.

We walked out to the car, and the night sky was perfectly black. The storm was rolling in and the winds preceding it only hinted at its force. "What's our plan?" Tom asked as he climbed behind the wheel.

"I thought we'd just walk in and wing it," I said.

"Wing it? You mean you don't have a plan?"

"Tom, a week ago I was a college student living a quiet life with my grandfather. Now I'm supposed to be a magical strategist?"

We both laughed and didn't discuss it further. There was no point in it. If this was indeed my destiny, it would play out as it was supposed to. On the other hand, Father Andrew and Tom and Simon—wherever he was—were trusting me with their lives. So many people had already died. That was when I remembered something from years before . . . my mother's name was Moira . . . it meant 'destiny' and it all clicked into place. *If Simon and the journal are right, that's who I am,* I thought. *Destiny's daughter.*

I cannot, must not, fail.

Sitting in the car across from the warehouse, I stared at the doorway and waited. There was no sign of Simon and the storm outside was getting worse by the minute. At last, I shrugged. "We can't wait for him any longer. We were supposed to be inside five minutes ago. If we don't show up soon . . ."

Tom agreed. "They might hurt Father Andrew worse than they already have."

"One thing first," I said. "I want to thank you."

"For what?"

"For helping me and . . . and for being my friend. You didn't have to stick by me through all this."

Tom grinned. "Yeah, well, I wanted to pound the life out

of Burke, but Simon beat me to it. Anyway, you weren't going anywhere tonight without me."

Knowing he was stronger than he looked, I smiled, and said, "I know. But thanks again."

"You're welcome, Jenna." We stared at each other for a moment, both of us thinking our own thoughts, and then he said, "Let's go."

I nodded and we both got out of the car.

The warehouse was old, with sheet metal that had once been painted a dark brown but had flaked away in many places. It looked like it was still being used, however, and that reassured me somewhat. An abandoned warehouse would have been a little too creepy. I saw light coming from beneath the door and shining through several of the windows, and as Tom and I crossed the street, the winds gusts made the metal siding creak and screech like fingernails on a chalkboard.

"Perfect," Tom muttered as we approached the door. "At least the sound effects are right."

"I'm trying to ignore it, thank you very much," I said. "Are you ready?"

He nodded. "Yeah, I guess," he said. "But before we go in, I wanted to tell you that—"

The door opened in front of us, interrupting Tom's words.

"You're late," the man standing there said.

"The lights were against us," I said. "Are you Peraud?"

The man laughed, sharp and bitter. "Hardly. I'm just the

hired help." He jerked his head toward the interior of the warehouse. "You were supposed to come alone," he said. "Who's he?"

"My bodyguard," I said. "Doesn't he look threatening?"

"Whatever," he said. "Let's go."

Wondering what Tom had wanted to say, I shrugged. "Okay."

We followed him inside and he led us through row after row of large crates stacked one atop the other almost to the ceiling. Most of them were labeled in black stencil: MACHINE PARTS! HEAVY! CARGO FORK LIFT ONLY! Like anyone would try to actually lift one by hand.

Near the center of the warehouse, a space had been cleared away for a worktable of some kind. A bare bulb in a protective metal shade hung down and cast its light on the table. The shadows surrounding us were thick and heavy, and I sensed several pairs of eyes watching us. Probably more of Peraud's lackeys, no doubt.

On the table was the Board. My Board. It rested on a velvet cloth and its call was so strong I could barely restrain myself from reaching out for it.

The man stopped near the table and said, "This is as far as we go." He pointed at the Board. "Touch it and all deals are off. Everyone dies."

"And I was just beginning to enjoy the scenery," I said. "Where's Father Andrew?"

A voice from the shadows said, "The Keeper at last." There

was pleasure in that voice, and yet, I sensed something more. "You were told to come alone."

I *felt* the voice more than heard it. It was the voice from the phone, but now unmodulated. Dark and heavy, like a moonless night or the inside of a tomb. And it was powerful. If felt like . . . I tried to think of something that the voice compared to and then I knew: it felt like the Board.

Trying to gather my wits, I said the first thing that came to mind, "I'm not one of your lackeys, Peraud. I thought you'd respect someone who played by the same rules you do— none at all." *Smooth, real smooth,* I thought.

"Unfortunate," the voice said. There was a moment of silence, and then, "Bring out the priest."

Two more men stepped forward from the shadows, carrying Father Andrew between them. He looked like he'd been beaten, but his eyes were bright. "Jenna," he said, his voice was exhausted. "You shouldn't have come."

"Be silent," one of the men said, cuffing him in the head.

"Stop it!" I cried. "Leave him alone!"

They propped him in a chair, where he slumped in exhaustion.

"There's your precious priest," Peraud said. "Now where is the journal?"

I motioned to Tom and he turned around. I opened his backpack and took out the journal. "Here," I said, holding it up. "The Chronicle of the Keepers."

The man stepped forward and the shadows moved with

him. I couldn't see his face at all, but only a dark silhouette of a human form. "Excellent," he said. "And our bargain?"

"Let Tom and Father Andrew go," I said. "When they are safely out of the warehouse, I will give you the journal and come with you quietly."

Peraud laughed, and I felt a frozen finger slide up my spine. "My dear girl," he said. "Why would I let *any* of you go? I have everything I want." The silhouette reached out and gestured and the journal flew out of my hands and through the air into his. He laughed again. "Now you will see real power, my girl."

"Let them go!" I yelled. "You don't need them. You have the Board, the journal, and me!"

"True enough," he said. "But in this day and age, I believe in—what is the phrase?—no loose ends." He turned to the men. "Kill the priest and the boy and bring the girl upstairs."

"You bastard!" I shouted, and that's when all the shadows around us moved at once.

"My Lord, I have the girl and the Board in my grasp, but she failed to come alone. Simon is also here—just as you predicted."

"Of course he is. I know him better than he knows himself. Finish it. Now. And if Simon gets in your way . . . well, you know what to do."

"Peraud!" a voice shouted from behind the crates.

The shadowy figure turned at the interruption and Simon stepped out into the light, along with several other men, all garbed in black clothing that had helped them hide within the warehouse. Their faces were covered, and only their calm eyes glittered in the dim light.

"Ah, the fallen priest," Peraud said, shaking his head. "I wondered when you'd show up." He gestured at the others. "And you've brought along some friends, I see."

"Throughout history, the Keeper has never truly walked alone," Simon said. "Give up the Board and the journal. We won't let you leave here with it."

Peraud laughed and clapped his hands together, the sound echoing loudly in the warehouse. Simon's eyes darted left and right as more and more of Peraud's men entered the open area, encircling myself, Tom and Simon and his men. "And who is going to stop me?" Peraud said. "You're outnumbered."

"Maybe," Simon said. "But not outgunned." He turned and looked at me. "Jenna, it's time."

Caught off guard, I said, "Time for what?"

Simon pointed at the Board. "Pick it up and fulfill your destiny," he said. "Call the winds."

Almost as though his words were commands, I felt myself take the first steps toward the Board. "My destiny," I whispered.

"Stop her!" Peraud shouted. "Now!"

The room exploded into action as everyone moved at once. Tom brushed by me, heading straight for Peraud, while several of the men surged toward me and the still groggy Father Andrew. I wanted to help Simon and Tom, but the Board was calling to me now. I heard it, as clear as I had in the visions.

"Call to me and I am yours."

I continued moving forward, ignoring the raging brawl going on around me.

"Call to me, Keeper. My power is yours to command."

I reached the table, my hand outstretched for the Board, but before I could grab it, I heard a sound that stopped me cold. Tom was screaming.

My head snapped around to look for him and I saw him, kneeling on the floor at Peraud's feet. He clutched his head in his hands, and his voice rose in a horrid shriek of pain. Peraud was laughing, holding a hand over his fallen enemy. My friend.

"Stop it! Leave him alone!" I yelled.

"Jenna!" Simon called. "You must get the Board!"

I turned and watched him backing away from two attackers, his hands loose at his side. He didn't look worried about the ensuing fight at all.

I had to use the Board and I tried to reach out with my mind. *"Help me! Bring the winds!"*

There was no reply, and it continued only to repeat its earlier plea: *"Call to me and I am yours."*

I didn't understand and the first stirrings of panic stirred in my belly. Two of Peraud's men grabbed Father Andrew and lifted him to his feet. They dragged him backward, striking him in his stomach and head as he struggled weakly to escape.

"Help me!" I mentally cried to the Board. *"Please!"*

"Call to me and I am yours."

Discouraged, I turned back to where Tom had been kneeling. Somehow, he had found the strength to get to his feet, though tears of agony streamed freely down his face. Gritting his teeth, I heard him say, "You . . . will . . . not . . . hurt . . .

her!" He lurched forward, trying to grab Peraud.

I felt my heart constrict as Peraud waved his hand nonchalantly. "Enough," he said.

Tom shrieked again and flew up into the air. Peraud flicked his long fingers again and Tom sailed into a stack of crates, smashing into them with bone-crushing force.

Stricken, I cried out as Tom fell to the floor, motionless. His face was ashen and he looked . . . he looked dead.

"NO!" I screamed. "Stop it!"

Peraud leapt toward me and before I could move, had me in his grasp. He spun me around to one side and wrapped a forearm around my throat. I still couldn't see his face, but his strength was evident. In my ear, he whispered, "Tell them to stop, or everyone that you love will die."

"Why are you doing this?" I asked, watching helplessly while Simon and the men he had brought with him were being outmatched.

"For power, of course," Peraud said. "Power that you will help me achieve. What else is there?"

"In your world," I said, "probably not a lot." I scanned the room and knew we were defeated. "Stop!" I yelled. "Simon, that's enough!"

Slowly, the combatants separated, all of them looking at me. Peraud kept his arm wrapped around my throat.

"That's it," I said. "We're done."

From the look of it, Simon had given a good accounting of himself. Several of Peraud's men lay on the floor, cradling injured limbs or out cold.

Peraud chuckled as the fighting came to a stop. "You're quite the warrior for a priest," he said to Simon.

"I grew up in an orphanage," Simon said, shrugging. "Even the Catholic ones are rough." Then his brow furrowed. "And I'm not a priest," he added.

"No," Peraud said. "You ran into some . . . difficulties with that, I understand."

"It's not your concern," he snapped. "Take the Board and the journal and go. Just leave Jenna here."

Simon was still trying to save me, and there was a feeling for me in his eyes that was undeniable.

"You're an educated man," Peraud said. "You know that without her, the Board and the journal are useless."

"Not true," Simon said. "If you wait, the Board will eventually sleep again, then *you* can reawaken it."

"You're willing to sacrifice all the people in this quaint little town to save her?" Peraud asked. He sounded genuinely intrigued. "That's not very noble at all."

"It's my choice," Simon said.

"While I admire your willingness to destroy others for your own desires," Peraud said, "I don't have time to wait. We're done here."

"Done?" I asked, wondering if he meant to let me go.

"Oh yes," he said. "Tanner!" he called. One of the men came out of the shadows near the closest stack of crates. "Your work here is almost done. Kill the priest and the hero, and make sure the boyfriend's dead, too, then meet me outside. We have a long journey ahead of us."

Tanner? I thought. *Burke's henchman? Why is he here?*

As if reading my mind, Peraud laughed. "Tanner works for me now," he said. "One of the things you'll soon learn is that everyone can be bought. Every soul is for sale." I felt his hand stroke my hair. "I wonder what your price is?" he whispered.

I felt his breath on my neck. The man was poisonous and evil. He had me, the Board, and the journal and he was going to kill Father Andrew, Simon . . . everyone. For his own pleasure.

His hand stroked my hair again and something inside me just . . . let go. I suddenly felt calm and in control. I knew what I had to do, how to save us all . . . if only there was time.

Closing my eyes, I thought about the Board on the nearby table, picturing it in my mind. The runes carved into its surface, the way it felt cold to the touch. I thought about Shalizander and how she had made the Board, driving the ornate dagger into its surface and bringing it to terrible life. I thought about power, and then I reached out and called:

"Board of the Winds, come to me. I am the Keeper, and your will is my will. Our hungers are the same and we are one!"

"I hear, Keeper," the Board called back. *"I hear and obey. What is your will?"*

I paused for a long moment, and I felt Peraud shift behind me. He still clutched the journal in his other hand. "What do you think you are doing?" he asked, his muscles tensing.

"What must be done," I said. I looked quickly at Simon, who nodded once and smiled. Then I reached out again: *"Release the storm."*

And the Board responded.

Outside the winds rose to a sudden shriek.

It sounded like the gates of Hell itself had been opened.

Ecstasy. The rush of power fills my blood, my lungs. I breathe in the magic of the Board. It surrounds and consumes me.

The winds are mine and I call to them, urging them on to greater heights and strength. Wanting them to come closer.

Shaking my head, I felt a rush of power so strong and intense that I felt like I was glowing like a neon light.

A voice shouted, "Peraud!" and I saw both him and Simon turn around in surprise.

A man I'd never seen before stepped into the light. He was dressed in an immaculate white suit and tie. He had dark skin and hair, with eyes that were almost black. He radiated strength and power, though he didn't appear to be much older than his mid-thirties.

Peraud released me. "Armand!" he said. "I assumed you would show up here. I've been waiting for you."

"Is that so?" Armand said. "My experience with you so far has lead me to believe you prefer sneaking around in the shadows to head-on confrontations."

"Perhaps once that was true," Peraud admitted. "But I'm much more powerful now. My master has seen to that."

"I sense that about you," Armand said. "But the question is, are you powerful enough?"

"There's only one way to find out," Peraud said as he released me. With a snarl on his face, he raised his hands and mumbled strange words under his breath.

"Indeed," Armand said.

Free, I stepped away from Peraud and turned around. He'd dropped the journal on the floor at his feet, and I picked it up. He saw me, but there was little he could do, distracted as he was by Armand.

I moved away from the two men just as a spinning ball of fire sprang out of Armand's outstretched hand. It expanded as it moved, and I thought Peraud would burn in agony, but he raised his arms, and the fire slammed into some kind of invisible wall that dissipated the flames harmlessly into the air.

In two quick strides, I reached the table and picked up the Board.

It felt like being I'd always imagined being in love would feel like, as though I were standing on the top of a mountain looking down on the world. I was Jenna Solitaire, but I would never be alone again, never be powerless again. Men like Burke and Peraud would never be able to harm me, or those I cared about. Never again.

"Peraud!" I screamed. "*I* am the Keeper of the Boards!" I raised my fist at him and pointed.

The Board knew my will before I had to command it. A

sudden, terrible shriek tore the roof from the warehouse. High above us, the lowering funnel of a massive tornado reached down from the sky. Men shouted and ran, scattering among the stacked crates, which were starting to shift in the incredible winds.

I heard a voice screaming my name, but I ignored it. The power was singing in me now, filling me with strength and resolve. I felt more alive than I ever had. I could not tell where the Board left off and I began. For the first time in my life, I wasn't powerless to stop people I cared about from being hurt.

Looking up, I saw the sky filling with funnel clouds, twisting and swirling around each other like angry black snakes. The winds pulled in sheets of rain and poured it down through the open roof of the warehouse in stinging pellets.

Peraud looked up and raised his own arms just as the fingertip of the tornado touched the stacks of crates, destroying each row as it sucked them into its voracious maw. Wood splinters flew everywhere, and I heard screams of agony. The lights flickered and popped, then went out.

"Power upon power. There is no end to it. I can dance on the clouds, float into the sky like a feather. I can see the lights of Heaven and below, the fires of Hell."

"Call upon me," the Board cries. "I have slept for so long and I ache to feel again, to use my strength again."

"Yes," I say. "I will use the Board! I will destroy the warehouse, Peraud and all of his men. I will save Armand, Simon, Tom and Father Andrew."

"They matter not," the Board says. "Destroy them all. You do not need them."

"Why?"

"You are powerful. You are the Keeper of the Winds, the Keeper of the Boards. You do not need anyone but me, my brethren, and the elemental power we can give you. Make them all kneel before you, and then destroy them."

"No!"

"Yes!"

The Board wants to . . . feed. It hungers for death and destruction. I must stop it. "No more! Take the winds away."

"Ah, the winds come at my command, but they disperse on their own. Our storm—the one you have created—is just beginning."

"NO!"

"YES!"

The first tornado touched down inside the warehouse and the ground trembled with the impact. The sides of the metal structure screeched, then blew out in a torrent of hundreds of fragments that whistled through the air like flying swords.

I saw Armand and Simon huddled together on the floor. Somehow the tornado hadn't touched them. Nearby, men were screaming and the air was filled with slivers of wood from the crates, clouds of razor-sharp metal darts from the warehouse walls, dust and debris. It was blinding and deafening . . . except where I stood. The Board kept me safe, the winds swirling around me in a maelstrom of devastation, but not touching me.

I couldn't stop the Board, and at that moment I wasn't even sure I wanted to.

Above us, several more funnel clouds snaked their way toward the ground.

I wondered where Peraud was, but he had disappeared.

I saw Armand gesture at Simon, who nodded and got tiredly to his feet.

He was screaming my name, I was sure of it, but I couldn't hear him.

I didn't want to hear him. Tom was dead, I was certain of it. And probably Father Andrew as well.

Simon had brought all of this into my life, and I was furious.

"Yes!" the Board cried in my head. *"They are to blame. Destroy them all!"*

Overflowing with power, but emotionally exhausted, I sank to the floor. I was the Keeper, but I couldn't control the Board. I didn't want to be angry anymore, didn't want to feel anything anymore.

"Please stop it," I said to the Board. *"Enough."*

"There is no such thing! We are power!"

Suddenly I saw the man from the cemetery standing in front of me. "You!" I said.

He nodded and dropped to his knees. "I work for Armand," he yelled, trying to be heard over the wind. "You must stop this! Control the Board!"

"I can't!" I screamed. "I won't!" I gestured and a tongue of wind whipped out and drove him to the ground. *Why had Armand sent someone to spy on me at my grandfather's funeral?*

Another man approached us, and even with his face cut and bleeding, I could see that except for a small mole on one cheek, he was almost identical to the man in front of me. Suddenly, I understood. Brothers or twins, and if one of them worked for Armand, then the other must work for Peraud!

He reached out and grabbed the other man by the ankles, began dragging him away from me.

I wondered if he was the one who'd broken into my house. Perhaps they meant me no harm all along. I didn't know, didn't care.

Out of the shadows, I saw the indistinct figure of Peraud. He was closing in on Armand and Simon. Apparently sensing the approach of his enemy, Armand turned to face him, shoving Simon in my direction.

The screech of the winds was horrific, a fearsome howl that reverberated through my very bones, and I wondered if anyone in the warehouse left alive would ever be able to hear again.

Simon staggered toward me, while the twins moved off into the storm in different directions.

I looked over to where Tom lay on the floor, fragments of wood and metal covering his clothes. He wasn't moving.

Nearby, Father Andrew was also on the floor, dropped earlier by his assailants when the storm hit and they panicked and ran. He was also still, and I saw blood on his forehead.

I rose to my feet, and the first thing I saw was real fear in Simon's eyes.

Even though I couldn't hear him over the winds, I could make out his words as he held up his hands, palms out, toward me. "Jenna! No!"

I ignored him, focusing instead on Armand and Peraud.

The two men faced off with each other, oblivious to the storm raging around them. Flickers of lightning, balls of fire, sprays of ice floated back and forth between them. For a moment, even I stopped to gasp in wonder. There was magic in our world, and almost no one knew about it. It was sad, in a way, and yet I also understood the reasons for it.

"They aren't magic! We are magic! They are charlatans compared to you and I!"

I knew this had to end, before the entire city was destroyed, but I didn't know how to stop it. I felt Simon take my arm and I turned to him. "What do I do?" I shouted, trying to make him hear me over the wind.

"You have to stop it!" he yelled. "Control the Board!"

"I can't! It's out of my control!"

"Everyone here will die if you don't!"

I tried to find some flicker of compassion in me, but the Board had smothered those feelings, replacing them with the singing exultation of power. I looked at Tom and Andrew again, and saw them as frail humans whose time in this life was at an end. I looked at Simon and shrugged, feeling myself grow colder inside. I didn't care; there was only the power of the Board coursing through me now. "Then they will die," I said. "It happens to everyone."

Simon grabbed me by the shoulders and I felt the Board's anger at him. "Is that what you want?" he screamed. "Is that what they would have wanted?" He pointed at Tom and Father Andrew. "For you to become a monster?"

"I am no monster!" I shouted, shoving him away from me. "I am power!"

The Board felt my anger and hurt and the winds ratcheted up even higher, to almost hurricane force. I heard other buildings in the town collapsing, and the distant wail of sirens rose and fell. Emergency workers were trying to get to the scene, but they would be too late.

Simon moved toward me again and before I could react, he slapped me—hard and fast—on one cheek. Stunned, I looked at him.

"Everyone here is trying to save you and you don't care. I may not be a priest anymore, but even I know that makes you a monster." Then he turned and staggered away toward Armand and Peraud.

"Is that what I am now? A monster?"

"No," the Board answered me. *"You are powerful—more powerful than any of them—and they are simply jealous."*

I looked over to where Armand and Peraud were trying to best each other. I glanced at Tom and Father Andrew and then I knew the truth of it. I wasn't a monster. I was hurt and scared to be alone in the world.

And the Board knew it.

It was playing on my worst fears.

"My Lord! She has lost control of the Board! She will destroy us all!"

"Peraud, you must listen to me. If you cannot contain her, then she must survive this. Do not let her die!"

"But for that to happen, she must not have a target for her anger."

"Then leave. There will be other opportunities later. She will fight all our battles for us, but we will win the war."

The storm raged through the warehouse, destroying everything in its path. The sky glowed the color of dark emeralds and lightning lit the funnel clouds swirling around in the night air. They reminded me of stylized dragons, twining about each other and fighting to the death.

If I couldn't control my fears, everyone here would die. The Board would keep calling the winds, exercising its long dormant powers and reveling in the destruction. Simon had said the Board was evil and conscious . . . and I knew he was right. If I didn't control the Board, it would control me. I would no longer be my own person.

What I didn't know is if I *could* control my fears. I hated the thought of being alone, of facing a destiny I knew nothing about . . . of losing my few friends. I missed my grandfather. I felt tears running down my face, and the sense of defeat that loomed over my thoughts was complete.

"Give yourself to me, Keeper. I will lift you up. I will protect you. You know I can do this. All you have to do is give yourself to me, and you need never fear anyone, anything again."

I gritted my teeth, trying and failing to block out the sound of the Board. I knew I would be hearing it for the rest of my days.

"You will never be alone."

Suddenly, I felt a hand on my shoulder and I turned around to see the last person I ever expected to see here— Kristen. Even in the furious winds and occasionally ducking the dangerous debris, she looked calm, poised even. "Jenna," she said. Even in her normal tone, I could hear her.

"Kristen? What are you doing here?"

"I came to find you. I could . . . feel you through the crystal I gave you. I don't know for sure what's going on with you right now, but you must stop this. You're destroying the city."

"It's not me!" I wailed. "It's the Board!"

"Perhaps," she said. "But to whom does the Board belong?"

That's when it hit me. My name was Jenna Solitaire, and I

had treated my whole life like that name defined my destiny. I had always thought I was supposed to be alone, never getting closer to anyone other than my grandfather. I wondered how Kristen had managed to get here, unharmed, through the storm. She obviously had powers of her own, and I felt her calm radiating around me, creating a sanctuary in which I could almost think straight.

"What do I do?" I said. "It's out of control!"

"No, Jenna," she said. "It's *you* who is out of control. The Board is only doing what it was made to do." She smiled, then, and said, "You haven't been alone, Jenna. All of us have been with you. You must choose to accept that, choose love and faith, and the rest will happen." Then she turned and made her way to where Tom had fallen, kneeling down beside him and covering his body with her own.

Although I hadn't thought it possible, the storm increased in intensity and I knew I had to do something right now. I glanced at where Peraud and Armand had been fighting and saw an exhausted-looking Armand straighten up, grimace in pain and then throw a strange cloud of heavy blackness at his opponent. It arched between them, growing and enveloped Peraud.

I saw him thrash about, like he'd been covered in some sort of inky skin, and then he broke through it and stepped out, the darkness shriveling into wisps of nothingness around him. His eyes were wide and fearful. He looked up at the sky and saw not one or two or even three, but dozens of tornadoes swirling above, ready to descend.

"Next time, Armand," he shouted, then turned and ran, calling for his men as he went.

Armand slumped to the ground, his once immaculate suit rumpled and stained.

Simon and I locked gazes, and he made his way back to me.

"Ignore him, Keeper. I am your friend."

"Simon," I shouted, trying to be heard above the howling winds. "Take my hand!"

He reached out and locked his hand around mine. "Jenna, please, you have to stop it!"

"I know," I said.

I reached out to the Board once more. I felt battered and drained now, like I'd been pummeled in an avalanche. *"You are not my friend! You are my* tool—*to use as I see fit!"*

"No!"

"Yes!" I screamed. *"And you will stop the winds—now! These are my friends!"*

Screeching in anger, the Board lashed out, and for a long minute, every tornado in the sky began lowering toward us.

"NO!" I commanded it. *"I choose them!"*

I looked at Simon, who had risked so much and asked only for me to be what I already was. I looked at Armand, who didn't even know me and had come to my aid. I looked at Tom and Kristen and Father Andrew and I knew the truth.

"I choose love," I said aloud.

"Yes, Jenna," Simon said, hearing me. "We can choose love and faith." He paused, and then added, "We always have."

His words rang a chord in me, and I knew then that somehow, somewhere or somewhen, we had known each other before. I wasn't sure how I felt about that, but it felt good to know that love was possible, even when the entire world around me seemed about to collapse.

"And you will *obey me,"* I added. *"I am the Keeper of the Winds."*

Defeated, the Board stopped raging, and replied, *"Yes, Keeper."*

Above us, the tornadoes reversed themselves, climbing back up into the sky. In minutes, the winds had stopped completely, and the clouds went with them, revealing a full moon and a bright blanket of spring stars.

The quiet was almost as noisy as the wind had been, and Simon stared at me with awe in his eyes. "You did it," he whispered.

I shook my head, looking at the devastation around us. Broken crates and slivers of sheet metal and parts littered the floor along with the bodies of those who hadn't escaped my wrath and the Board's magic. "No," I said. "*We* did it."

Simon and I waited for the emergency people to arrive—fire trucks, police cruisers and ambulances rushed into the area as soon as the winds died down. The sirens, flashlights and rushing men and women were enough to make me want to run and hide, but Simon calmed me down. "We have to play along with this charade, Jenna," he said. "At least until we can get out of here. Just follow my lead."

As battered and tired as all of us were, Simon's story was simple enough: Kristen, Tom, Simon and I were driving by the area when the storm hit and decided to take shelter in the warehouse. What we didn't know was that some kind of criminal activity—he gestured to Peraud's men, including the unconscious Tanner—was going on. From what little we heard before the storm hit, it appeared that Father Andrew had been kidnapped and was going to be ransomed. Fighting broke out when we tried to escape at the height of the storm, and Tom and Father Andrew were injured.

I watched as both of them were loaded onto stretchers and into the back of an ambulance. As she walked by, Kristen gave me a small smile and whispered, "You did it right, Jenna. Good for you."

Watching them load Tom into the ambulance, I didn't feel like I'd done much of anything right, but Kristen had proven beyond a doubt that she was my friend, too, so I nodded at her and tried my best to smile back. She climbed into the ambulance with Tom and I watched it start to drive away.

Father Andrew, it appeared, had only sustained minor injuries—lots of bruises and cuts, as well as a dislocated shoulder—but the paramedics were able to bring him around quickly.

Tom had not fared nearly as well. He was still unconscious, and from the way they strapped him down, I thought maybe he had a broken neck . . . or worse.

The police asked us a few more questions, but they were in a hurry to wrap up here and move on to other areas of the city that had been damaged during the storm. One of them said that if we thought of anything else, we should give them a call. Otherwise, they'd be in touch.

As the ambulances pulled out, I picked up the Board and put it back in its case. I still heard it calling softly to me, but now it was muted and under control. I slid it into Tom's backpack and added the journal, vowing silently to myself to figure out exactly how the Board worked and how to control it.

Then I turned to Simon and said, "Drive me to the hospital?"

He nodded. "Sure," he said. "Let's go."

We stepped out of the ruins of the warehouse and into a surprisingly warm early spring night.

Miller's Crossing could not boast of many things, but it had a good hospital staffed by solid doctors. When Simon and I got there, however, they were completely overwhelmed. Between the injuries and destruction from the night before, and now this storm, the staff was stretched to the limit. Apparently, a small plane had also tried to leave the area and been caught in the horrendous winds and crashed, killing everyone on board when it slammed into a small apartment building, injuring dozens of others. For once the usual hospital scents of disinfectant and floor cleaner were overwhelmed by the smells of the injured. It wasn't a pleasant trade.

It took a while for us to even figure out where Father Andrew and Tom had been taken. When we did, I told Simon that we should see Father Andrew first.

We found him propped up in bed, sharing a room with two other patients, and reading the bedside Bible. He saw us and smiled. "Jenna!" he said. "Simon! It's good to see you both alive and well."

"Father," I said, taking his hand. "Are you all right?"

"I'm fine," he said, "so long as I don't shrug my shoulder too much. Otherwise, it's mostly damage to my pride." He winked at Simon. "I'm not the battler I once was in my youth."

"You?" I asked, incredulous. "I can't imagine you fighting with anyone!"

"Simon can," he said. "Can't you, my friend?"

Simon grinned. "As I said, growing up in a Catholic orphanage is *tough*," he replied. "But we did okay, didn't we?"

"Yes, we did," Father Andrew replied.

I felt my jaw hinge open and Simon reached out and lifted it back up with his finger. "Yes, Jenna," he said. "Father Andrew spent some time at the same orphanage I did. He was quite a bit older than I was and was one of the first kids to beat me up." He laughed. "I admired him."

Father Andrew chuckled. "You turned out all right, Simon," he said. "I see you managed to hold on to your birthright."

Simon touched the coin necklace lightly and smiled. "If you couldn't take it from me in the orphanage, then no evil sorcerer or conjured tornadoes could."

"No," Father Andrew replied. "I suppose not. Then his face

grew serious. "Jenna, I don't know what all is really going on—Simon can't or won't tell me, and that's his prerogative—but I can tell you that he's a good man and won't harm you."

I nodded. "I know," I said. "But that doesn't make all this any easier to swallow."

"You and Simon are a lot alike, you know," the priest said. "Both of you have lost your faith in so many ways." He sighed, and then held up a hand before either of us could respond. "It's possible that if you work together, you both may find it again."

Not wanting to say more or dash his hopes, I just nodded, and Simon smiled, holding out his hand and shaking with his old friend.

"Now get going," Father Andrew said. "I'm tired and could use a nap. Plus, I suspect you want to go find Tom."

"Yes," I said. "Rest well, Father. I'm glad you're okay."

"The Lord protects the faithful, Jenna," he said. "Even in the darkest of hours."

"Does he?" I asked. "Even then?"

"Especially then," he said. "Take care of yourself, Jenna, and hold fast to the light of the truth." He looked at Simon. "You'll be leaving soon, I suspect?"

"Tomorrow or the day after," he said. "As soon as she's ready to go."

"Me?" I asked. "Where am I going?"

Simon grinned. "I'll explain it to you later, okay?" He took Father Andrew's hand again. "Be well, my friend. God keep you safe."

"You, too, Simon," Father Andrew said.

"Goodnight, Father," I said, and we stepped quietly out of the room, leaving him to his much needed rest.

The hallways were chaotic, with staff rushing everywhere as we made our way up to the ICU where Tom was. Kristen stood outside his room, anxiously looking in through the glass, but she must have seen us coming, because she turned to greet us.

I gave her a hug, holding tight to her and feeling her incredible warmth. "How is he?" I asked.

A frown marred her features. "It's not good," she said, trying not to cry. "Both . . . both of his legs are broken, along with some ribs. And . . . they say he's paralyzed, Jenna. He took a good blow to the head, too, and he's in a coma. They don't know . . . they don't know if he'll wake up or not."

"Oh, Kristen," I said. "I'm so sorry."

"It's not your fault, Jenna," she said, sniffling. "He wanted to go with you."

"I should have figured it out faster," I said, trying to hold back my own tears. "I should have protected him better."

"He would never have stood for it," she said. "He liked being your hero."

"And he is," I said. "He's also my best friend."

"I know," she said. "And you are his."

Without warning, a shrill beeping sound came from Tom's room. Several nurses rushed past us, and one of them shouted, "Page the doctor, he's coding."

"What . . . what does that mean?" Kristen whispered.

I didn't answer her because I knew that she already knew

the answer. I felt my stomach clench and turn to ice. My best friend was dying . . . and it was all my fault.

The beeping sound changed tones as the doctor ran past.

From inside the room, I heard a nurse yell, "He's flat-lining. Get that cart going!"

Kristen reached out blindly for my hand and I took it. We were going to lose him . . . and there wasn't anything I could do about it.

I turned around to look for Simon and he was gone. "Where . . . ?" My voice trailed off as I looked through the window into Tom's hospital room. Somehow, in the midst of the chaos, Simon had found a way through the nurses and doctors.

They didn't even seem to notice him, but I couldn't imagine how they missed him. He . . . *glowed* . . . with an inner light of some kind. Everything . . . slowed down, and while I could feel Kristen's grip in mine, could see the doctor and the nurses moving and talking, it was like watching time pass one very long second at a time.

Simon reached out and grasped Tom's slack hand, and closed his eyes. His lips moved, and I knew he was praying. Praying for Tom and for a miracle of some kind.

I wanted to pray, too, but . . . something inside held me back. I could only watch in amazement as another light, silver and bright, came down from the ceiling.

The hospital staff didn't even blink, and Simon continued to hold Tom's hand and pray with his eyes shut tight. Everyone kept working, and I vaguely heard the sound of the doctor yelling, "Clear!" as they tried to jolt Tom back into this world.

The light drifted down and settled over Simon and then . . . expanded outward to cover Tom's still form.

"Clear!" the doctor yelled again.

The silver light—*presence?* I wondered—grew brighter at the same moment, and everything sped up again.

"He's back, doctor," one of the nurses said. Then she turned and noticed Simon standing there, holding Tom's hand. "How'd you get in here?" she asked.

Simon didn't answer, he just backed quietly out of the room, the glow surrounding him fading away even as he moved.

"Kristen," I whispered. "Did you see that?"

Smiling, crying, she said, "Yes, thank the goddess. They brought him back."

She hadn't seen it, then. "Simon prayed for him," I said.

"He did?" she asked as Simon stepped out of the room. "You did?" she said to him.

He looked tired and careworn as he gazed back into the room where Tom was now sleeping. "Yes," he said softly. "I prayed for him. It was the least I could do."

"Thank you," Kristen said. "I'm not a Christian, but thank you."

"It was my pleasure," Simon replied, then he gently took my arm. "Come on, Jenna," he said. "Tom looks like he's in good hands now."

I followed him outside, where for a long time both of us said nothing.

"Simon," I finally managed, "How did you do that?"

He looked at me, his head cocked to one side in confusion. "Do what?" he asked.

"Heal Tom like that?"

Simon laughed. "Heal him? What are you talking about? I only offered a prayer—actually the Sacrament of the Sick."

"Simon, you *healed* him," I insisted. "I saw the whole thing."

"Jenna, you've been under a lot of strain lately, and we don't have any idea of the precise nature of the Board's powers. I did *no such thing*."

I didn't know why but either Simon had no memory of what happened in Tom's hospital room or he didn't want to believe it. Either way, *I* had seen the truth. Simon was a true man of God . . . and he'd somehow lost his way. Another mystery to be figured out.

"Okay," I said. "But it was pretty amazing to see him come back like that."

"Faith," Simon said, smiling softly. "Combined with good medical technology. Together, they can work miracles."

"I'm beginning to think there may be more to faith than technology," I muttered. "Maybe a lot more."

Simon shrugged. "Let's go see about some food and some rest," he said. "We can talk more about it tomorrow."

We found some bad food in the cafeteria and tried to sleep in the lounge while we waited for news about Tom's condition. Kristen wandered in from time to time, looking like a ghost, but keeping her vigil.

Around mid-morning, Tom's doctor gave us the news: "I've never seen anything quite like it," he said. "We were sure he was gone, and then he just . . . came back. There's still the paralysis to deal with, but . . . in time, well, he'll do fine."

"Can we see him?" Kristen asked.

The doctor nodded, but said, "Keep it brief, okay? He's going to be groggy for a couple of days and needs his rest." We promised to do so, and he walked out of the room, shaking his head.

We went into Tom's room and Kristen and I stood on either side of Tom's bed. Simon stood in the doorway, looking more priest-like and somber than ever.

Tom's eyes flitted open and he did his best to smile up at us. "Glad to see you're all alive," he whispered.

"Which one of us?" I asked. "I almost got you killed."

"Yes, but I would have won," he said, his voice a mere croak.

"Won?" I asked. "How?"

"You bought . . . our last coffee."

Remembering a long ago conversation between us, I started laughing. His sense of humor was still intact anyway.

Kristen said, "I don't get it."

I quickly explained that Tom and I had a long-running bet between us that on the day one of us died, the other would have bought the last round at the coffee shop, preventing the other from evening out the debt. "I said there was no way that could happen, and he said it was practically guaranteed." I shrugged. "Guess there is such a thing as destiny after all."

"There sure is," Kristen said. "Right now, his fate is to rest. It will be days and days before he gets out of here, and *I'm* not bringing him a coffee!"

Tom tried to laugh, but it sounded more like a dying cat than anything else. He grimaced with the pain. His eyes were cloudy with it, but he stared at me intensely. "You've got to go now, don't you?" he asked.

I nodded. "Yes, I think so. Simon hasn't made it all clear yet, but I'm pretty sure I'll be leaving for awhile."

"Stay in touch?" he asked.

"Always," I said. I gestured at his backpack. "I've got your Blackberry."

"Figures," he said.

"Take care, Tom," I said. "And thanks. Thanks for everything and for being my friend. You are a hero."

"No," he said. "I just love you."

"I know," I said. "Take care of him, Kristen, and yourself, too."

"I will," she said. "You, too."

Feeling a familiar set of eyes on me, I glanced at the door where Simon stood, waiting for me patiently. "I better go," I said. "My life, I think, isn't completely my own anymore."

"No one's ever is, Jenna," Tom whispered. He was starting

to fall asleep and Kristen held his hand. "We all belong to each other."

I smiled and then slipped out of the room to where Simon waited.

Together, we left the hospital and he drove me home.

The ride home was quiet, neither of us saying anything. Simon walked me to my front door, then paused and said my name.

I turned back to face him, my hand on the doorknob. "I'm tired, Simon," I said. "No more for tonight, okay?"

"I know, Jenna," he said. "I only have two things to say."

"What?" I asked, dreading that he might say words that he couldn't take back.

"I'm proud of you," he said. "Armand told me that he thought you would make an excellent Keeper."

"And?" I said.

"You need to be careful," he reminded me. "The Board is extremely powerful and it is already calling to the next Board. If you listen, you might even be able to hear it answering."

"I'll listen for it later," I said. "Right now, I just need to sleep."

Simon nodded. "Goodnight, Jenna," he said. Then he turned and walked back to his car. I watched him drive away and wondered if I should have invited him inside.

"You don't need him," the Board whispered in my mind. *"You have me. You will always have me."*

Ignoring it, I went inside and locked the door behind me, hoping that dreamless sleep would come . . . and knowing that it wouldn't.

15

"You are certain she will be leaving, my Lord?"

"She cannot help it. The next Board is calling to her, and she has no choice but to answer. At last, this one, untrained girl, will accomplish what five thousand years of effort could not. And we will be there for it!"

Water rushes toward me in a wall . . .

A tsunami dances on the surface of the sea . . .

Cresting, it plunges down over me and I taste salt and death . . . a strange thrumming beat fills the air. It calls to me. The Board of Water. That is the next Board and I can hear it in my mind, my skin . . . my heart.

Where . . . somewhere far from home . . . to the desert . . . to a place where kingdoms rose and fell on scimitars blooded by Christians and heretics . . .

"Come to me . . . Call me and I will be yours . . ."
I am in the water and everything around me is dead . . .

I sat up in bed, feeling worse than I had the night before when I fell asleep. I knew that today would be my last day in Miller's Crossing, and while I had always wanted to travel, the circumstances that had made that possible weren't exactly what I'd had in mind.

After dragging myself out of bed and through my morning routine, I sat in the living room, wondering how long it would take before Simon showed up and demanded that we leave. I shrugged—why wait for him when I had other things to do? It wasn't like he'd had trouble finding me before.

Outside, last night's promise of spring was being fulfilled. The sun shone, the puddles of rain from last night's storm were drying up and birds were singing in the trees. I stepped to the front door and opened the hall closet to get a light jacket. The suitcase was gone and I realized that Simon must have taken it when he left the day before. I wondered what he'd done with the money, then realized I didn't really care.

Has it only been a day? It feels like a year.

I pulled my backpack over my shoulder, and realized that for the foreseeable future, there would never be a day when I wouldn't carry the Board and the journal with me. To leave them behind was unthinkable—so many people had paid with their lives for me to have them—and yet . . . I couldn't use the Board either.

I knew that it would always want to exercise its powers and that was a risk I couldn't take again. The power had felt too good, too seductive.

Stepping into the sunlight, I realized that I didn't have a car—Simon had taken it, I guessed—then shrugged and began walking toward St. Anne's. I wanted to say good-bye to my grandfather and grandmother before I left. I had no idea when I'd be back.

It was a good day for walking. The day was warm and a soft, natural breeze blew from the south. It smelled fresh and clean, and a vague scent of early grass wafted from the ground. Wishing I would get to see the garden this summer, I rounded the corner and made my way to the church.

Father Andrew would still be in the hospital, of course, though I guessed that they wouldn't be able to keep him there for very long. He'd be back giving Mass and taking confessions within a few days, a week at the most.

St. Anne's came into sight and I walked into the gardens planted and cared for by my grandmother and the grounds maintained by my grandfather. I wended my way through statues and headstones, and thought about how lucky I was that Tom and Kristen and Father Andrew had survived. I would stay in touch with them as often as I could. Good friends were too rare and valuable to discard like yesterday's newspaper.

The headstone where my grandparents were buried had

been washed clean by the wind and the rains. My parents' headstone, too. I knelt down between the plots and saw that someone had brought flowers—they were still fresh—and placed a bouquet in front of each stone. I wondered if a neighbor had done it, when I felt a presence behind me.

I knew who it was and didn't turn around. "Good morning, Simon."

"Good morning, Jenna. Were you able to get some rest?"

"Not very much," I admitted. "Somehow I doubt Keepers ever do."

"Probably not," he said. "I brought the flowers for you. I knew you didn't have a car."

"Thanks," I said. "They're lovely."

"Jenna, I spoke to Armand this morning," Simon said.

"And?"

"He is curious to know if you will . . . if you plan on serving good or evil."

"I don't understand," I said. "I didn't know I had to serve anyone or anything."

"The Boards are evil, Jenna. The role of the Keeper in many ways is to be the force that resists that evil. Peraud wants them for his own foul uses. Why do *you* want them?"

I stood up and brushed my hands on my jeans. "Simon, I don't want them. I have to do this. I accept that this is my destiny, whether I want it or not. I don't serve good or evil, or Peraud or Armand. I'm not going to be a part of this war."

"You *are* a part of this war," he said.

I shook my head. "No, Simon, I'm not. I serve me. I am the Keeper of the Boards and I may be coming into my knowledge a bit late, but I think all of you have oversimplified this a bit. This isn't about good or evil . . . it's about power and how it is used. The Boards were made for a specific purpose."

"They were?" Simon said, eyebrows raised. "How do you know that?"

"I can feel it," I said. "Now leave me alone to say my goodbyes. I'll meet you at the car."

"Very well," he said. He turned and walked back across the cemetery to where he'd parked my grandfather's car.

I waited until he was out of earshot, then looked at the graves of my family. "I don't know when I'll be back," I said. "Maybe never. But I love you and miss you. I'd give anything to know that you were with me, but more than that, I hope all of you are at peace." I blew a kiss to each headstone, then turned and walked away.

Long good byes never serve a real purpose except to delay the pain of leaving. But the pain comes anyway.

Simon was waiting for me and he drove me back to the house. The whole way there, he remained silent, and I was thankful for that—and that he didn't say a word about my tears.

Sitting at the kitchen table, Simon said, "Where are we going?"

I sipped my coffee and thought of my vision from the

night before. "The Middle East," I said. "Jerusalem, I think, near the Dead Sea. But I thought you probably knew that."

"Not exactly," he said. "The last clue I found to the Board of Water led me to believe it was in the Caribbean, perhaps the Bahamas."

I shook my head. "No, it's over there somewhere. I can feel it."

"Okay," he said. "We have to leave, tonight if we can. Tomorrow at the latest."

"Why are we in such a rush?" I asked.

"Because what if Peraud can hear the Board calling, too?" Simon asked. "We don't know that he can, but we don't know that he can't. Armand said he's much more powerful than he was the last time they met. We don't want him to get to it before we do."

"Point taken," I said. "Still, I've got to arrange for finances and the house and my belongings. That's going to take some time."

"Not really," Simon said. He reached into his coat pockets and pulled out a sheaf of papers. "Here's an updated statement of your checking account, along with some other papers you'll need to sign."

I quickly scanned them and saw that my current checking account balance was . . . my eyes widened. Over fifty thousand dollars. "Where did you—?" I snapped my mouth closed and saw that Simon had put more money into a dividend paying mutual fund. That money, along with what was regularly deposited from my parents and grandparents' trusts would take care of my needs comfortably for years.

"Why?" I asked.

"We're going to need the money," he said. "Why not use it for good instead of evil?"

I agreed and said, "What about the house? I'd planned on selling it, even though I didn't want to."

"I guessed that," he said. "But you shouldn't sell it. It's your home and you may want to come back here someday. It's always good to have a place to come home to."

"Who will take care of it?"

There was a knock on the door and Simon grinned. "That should be her now," he said. "I'll be right back." He got up from the table and a moment later I heard Kristen's voice calling my name.

"Jenna! Are you serious about this?"

I looked at Simon. "Of course she is," he said. "Who better to stay here and take care of things than one of her best friends? Besides, Tom is going to need a place to recuperate and he can't do it going up and down the steps to his apartment, right?"

"Right," I said, knowing that Simon had made a good decision.

"Yes, but Jenna, we should at least pay you something," Kristen said.

I shook my head and smiled. "You already have," I said. "Your friendship is payment enough and it's not like the house costs me anything. The mortgage was paid off years ago. Just keep up with the utility bills, okay?"

"Agreed," she said. "Thanks so much! This will make school a lot easier, too!" She was very excited and I could see that she was just aching to tell Tom, but there was something I had to ask her about first.

"Kristen," I said, "I'm wondering about something."

"What's that?" she asked.

"The crystal you gave me. The story about the love spell you cast on Tom. All of it, I guess. How much power do you really have?"

Kristen laughed softly. "Not enough to threaten yours," she said. "I'm just a small town witch, really."

"So how come you never said anything when Tom and I were making fun of you? Why didn't you tell us?" I really wanted to know because Tom and I had teased her mercilessly.

She looked around the house and gestured vaguely. "Before all of this, would you have believed me?"

I laughed and shook my head. "Probably not," I admitted. "But I still feel bad."

"Don't," Kristen said. "In a small town like this, I prefer the anonymity—and that's something I don't think you're going to get the luxury of having." She leaned closer in and added, "There is one thing, though . . ."

"What's that?" I asked, putting a hand on her shoulder and hugging her close.

"Tom doesn't really know about my true abilities and I'd

kind of like to keep it that way. So . . . would you mind not saying anything to him about it?"

Tom, I thought, *you are going to have your hands very full.* "He won't hear a peep out of me," I promised.

"Thank you," Kristen said. She gestured around the kitchen. "For everything. No matter where you travel, Jenna, Tom and I will always be your friends and we'll always be with you."

"You're welcome," I said. "Now why don't you go tell Tom about it?" I suggested. "He's probably ready for some company anyway."

"Yeah," Kristen said. "Besides, I've been reading to him out of this new book I got." She held it up so I could see it. The cover was some kind of weird shiny chromatic swirl of color and read: PAST LIVES AND THE LOVERS WHO LIVED THEM. "He loves it," she said.

Chuckling, I said, "I bet he does. Take care of yourself, Kristen."

"You, too, Jenna," she said. "Thanks again." She clasped me in a tight hug, and added a whispered, "Be careful out there," before heading back out the front door.

I didn't say anything to Simon for a long minute after she left, and then I smiled. "Good choice," I said.

"They deserve it," he replied. "And now I have to use your phone. We have plane tickets to buy and a lot to do before tomorrow."

"I know," I said. "I'll go pack."

I went upstairs and began putting my life into a suitcase

227

and looking around my room, wondering if I would ever see it again. The art prints on the walls, the little white vanity my grandfather had given me when I turned sixteen, my comfortable reading chair and the small desk next to it where I had done more homework than I could remember. I ran a hand along the quilted comforter that my grandmother had made—a stars and moons pattern. Reminders of my past life, and that it was gone as inevitably as my family.

I doubted I would ever see any of it again.

This would always be where a piece of my heart was, I knew, but I was the Keeper of the Boards, and home would be wherever I needed to be to find the next one and keep it safe.

"Miss, can I get you anything else?" the flight attendant asked.

"Not right now," I said. "Thank you."

She nodded and continued to pass through the first class cabin. Simon had balked at spending the money, but I badgered him about it until he gave in. "It's a long flight," I told him. "We have the money and may as well be comfortable."

He'd finally agreed, but I guessed he felt unused to such treatment. He kept scowling every time the poor woman came by and offered us anything.

The backpack containing the Board and the Chronicle of the Keepers was under the seat in front of me, and I glanced at Simon, who appeared to be asleep. "Simon?" I said. "Are you awake?"

"Yes," he said quietly. "But I'd *like* to sleep. I'm tired."

"That makes two of us," I said. "But I can't sleep."

He opened his eyes. "What's the problem?"

"I'm afraid to sleep. Every time I do, I see things, dream things and it's always me as someone else."

"Are you experiencing your past lives as the Keeper?" he asked.

"I don't think so," I said. "I think I'm just experiencing their lives as they lived them. I don't think it was me, really, it just feels that way."

"You should consider it an opportunity to learn," he said firmly. "Maybe it will give you information you need."

"Maybe," I said. "But that's not what I'm worried about."

"Then what is it?" he asked.

"Not all of the Keepers were . . ." My voice trailed off as I tried to find the right word and failed.

"Were?" he prompted.

"Nice," I finally said. "Many of them, I think, were as mad for power as the Boards themselves. They were like Peraud."

"They made their choices, too, just as you did in the warehouse," Simon said. "Some of them chose to use the Boards. You should not unless you absolutely have to."

"Because they are evil?" I asked.

"Yes," he said. "But more than that, because of the power they represent."

"You mean what they can do?"

"No," he said. His face was solemn. "Armand and I believe that they may be connected to some sort of demon or evil entity not of this world. The Boards may derive their power from that force, and not any natural magical source."

"A demon?" I said. "They really exist?"

Simon sighed. "Without a doubt," he said. "They are angels of evil."

"You've seen one?" I asked.

His scowl deepened and he said, "No more questions right now, Jenna. We can talk more after we get some sleep. The important thing is that you remain true to who you are, who your grandfather raised you to be—a good person trying to do her best—and that you accept your destiny as the Keeper of the Boards." He leaned his seat back and closed his eyes. "Now try to get some sleep."

I didn't answer him, but I thought about what he said for a long time. Was it even possible to be the Keeper *and* a good person? Why had I been chosen to have this destiny? Why not my mother or my grandmother or some other Solitaire woman at some point in the past?

I looked at Simon who was breathing softly. He had already fallen asleep. He was a man with secrets, too, and I realized that while I cared for him, I didn't fully trust him either. I would have to make sure to use my own judgments and instincts when we got to Jerusalem and began searching for the next Board.

I'd never been to the Middle East, and I was excited to see it. The desert was supposed to be beautiful, and the Dead Sea had been the site of so many historic events. I could not see the future, and my past was as different from that and my present as could be. In some ways, I missed Miller's Crossing already, but in others, it had been good to leave. I felt horrible for the death and destruction that had come to my home and the quiet people who lived there. So many had paid with their lives because I had refused to face the truth and I would be thinking about that, I knew, for many days to come.

Simon was right. I was the Keeper—for good or for ill—and it was my destiny. Someday, perhaps, I would figure out why.

I picked up the backpack and removed the journal, ignoring the Board's voice in my head, constantly whispering to me, asking me to call on it. So far, every time I'd read the Chronicle, it had exhausted me, and I silently wondered if reading it was completely safe. Still, I had to have information if I was going to survive and learn what I needed to know. If there was a danger to it, it was a risk I was willing to take.

Leaning back in my seat, I opened the journal to the front and watched as the letters rearranged themselves into readable English. Simon had told me that only the Keeper could read it—to all others, it was an undecipherable mess often called the Language of the Birds . . . the language of man before the fall of the Tower of Babel.

The first lines of the journal read:

To my daughters,
I am sorry for the burden you will inherit, but judge me not harshly. I tried to save us all and failed. The future of the world depends on you and preventing one thing: the opening of the way.

May this journal guide you and all your heirs until the Daughter of Destiny arrives and masters the Boards.

Your mother,
Shalizander

As I read, the gentle motion of the plane rocked me to sleep, her words and the words of the other Keepers . . . and the Boards, always the Boards . . . whispering in my ear.

EPILOGUE

"My Lord, what you propose is a dance with the Devil."

"No, Peraud. It is a chance to conquer the universe, and make the Devil himself kneel before us."

The gardens are lush and ripe. A maze of plant life hangs over carved pathways and ancient stones. Fruit blossoms and fern leaves fill the air with the scent of summer.

I wait for him in a small grotto.

We meet here often, after our work is done. When the moon is at its apex and the plants above bathe in its soft silver light. I feel him coming toward me. His steps are steady and sure and eager.

He enters the grotto, but does not speak my name. It is one of our rules. Here we do not speak to each other. Here we do not know anything of each other or worry about the work we do.

In this place, we are only spirits and flesh. Our voices are given only in longing.

The night is humid and as he approaches, I see the beading sweat on his brow, the flex of his muscles beneath his robe. I inhale, taken by the sight of him, his stern countenance in the moonlight.

He comes closer and with steady hands lifts me up, and carries me to a bench that I covered with a blanket. It has been many days since our work has allowed us to be together and I shiver in anticipation.

After setting me down, he turns around and picks up the bowl of grapes I brought. I see the mark on his shoulder—a birthmark, he once told me—that is shaped like a star with nine rays. It glistens in the moonlight, and not for the first time I wonder if he spoke the truth about it. I wonder if the mark means something more.

He turns back and sits beside me, popping the skin of a grape between his teeth. Lowering his mouth to mine, he kisses me, and I taste the flavor of the grape on his lips. They are lush, ripe and red, and the juice is sweet on my tongue.

In the light of the stars, it looks like blood as he takes another grape and squeezes it between his strong fingers, letting the juice run into my open mouth. His eyes sparkle as he places a kiss on my neck and I feel myself gasp in response.

But I do not speak.

Once, I broke our rule and spoke to him. Without a word,

he turned away from me and left the grotto. I waited for him until the sun rose and I had no choice but to return to my rooms. I have never again spoken to him here.

I open my mouth once more and he feeds me grapes, one by one. Their sweetness pops on my tongue like reminders of spring wine. Above, I see the moon shining down and the leaves of the plants. The humid air makes me sweat and the sting of it on my skin reminds me of the bittersweet magic we share, our dream of creating items so powerful we can use them to conquer the world.

Earlier today, we finished the last of our preliminary research. The items could be made in the form of Boards. Getting the materials would take time and much strength, but it could be done . . . and those tasks would seem simple compared to the danger of weaving of the spells required to make the Boards work.

The energy between us is almost palpable and with a wave he summons it out of the air. Currents of psychic energy, like small bolts of lightning, arc between us.

He kisses me, and in my mind I can hear his voice.

"Our vision shall be made real—the power will be infinite . . . and ours."

I kiss him back, running a hand over his star-scarred shoulder.

"Yes." *I will share his vision and power, helping him craft the Boards into items of earth-shattering magic.*

"Yes." *My heart and his, our souls, are one.*

I tell him all this, with my mind and he has no choice.

He says, "Yes."

Beneath the plants and the moon and the stars, we know that the future belongs only to us and the magic we create . . . together.

ACKNOWLEDGMENTS

Without the kindnesses of Martin H. Greenberg, John Helfers, Larry Segriff, and Susan Chang, my story would never have been shared with all of you. If you run into them somewhere and you enjoyed reading this, thank them for bringing these pages into the world. Special thanks also to Sherri, who helped shape the vision and shared coffee on so many nights. If you run into her, buy her a Starbucks.

ABOUT THE AUTHOR

Jenna Solitaire was raised in Ohio, and now lives the life of a vagabond, searching the world for the next Board. When she was nineteen, she learned that she was the Keeper of the Boards, and her life has been filled with magic and mayhem ever since. With Simon Monk, she continues to travel the world and learn about the Boards of Babylon. She believes that sharing her story with others is important and plans on continuing to do so for as long as she can. Her next journey is chronicled in Book 2: THE KEEPER OF THE WATERS and she hopes you enjoy reading it.

Please visit her website at www.tor.com/jennasolitaire for updates about her adventures, to read her blog entries, or to send her an e-mail. She'll try to answer you if she can.

See below for a preview from
Daughter of Destiny #2:

KEEPER
OF THE
WATERS

coming soon from Tor Teen!

"Simon! Jenna!"

I turned to see Armand waving and calling our names. He was dressed in a white linen suit coat and pants, and looked much more at home in this climate than he had in Ohio. We crossed through the throngs of people coming out of customs, a dozen different languages being spoken, shouted, or whispered all around us. The clash of noises and smells was overpowering, so I focused on dragging my suitcase over to where Armand was waiting.

As we got closer, I saw another man standing next to Armand. His hair was jet black and pulled tightly into a long ponytail, his skin the color of coffee with a touch of cream. . . . But it was his eyes that affected me the most; a deep amber color, almost golden, that locked onto mine with a jolt of recognition. I felt my stomach constrict, like I'd seen this man somewhere before, and the recognition between us was a physical thing, as natural as sunrise.

My stomach fluttered and my hands went numb, which was when I lost my grip on my suitcase. I stooped to pick it up, and he was right beside me. His hand covered mine for a moment I wanted to go on forever, and then released it. He had a masculine, smoky scent about him that I wanted to drink in with every breath.

"May I help you, Miss Solitaire?" he asked. His voice was as deep and smooth as a river. Dressed in pressed black slacks and a white, raw cotton shirt that emphasized his shoulders and was open at the neck, he was striking in the same way some male models are—you couldn't help but look. My eyes went up to meet his, and I realized that he stood a good four inches taller than I was, which meant he was at least 6' 2".

"How do you . . . " I started to say, when Armand's cultured voice interrupted. To me, his voice sounded like it was meant for reading old fairy tales aloud.

"Ahh, Jenna," he said. "I see you've met our guide. This is Saduj Nomed." He nodded at Simon's questioning look.

"Yes," he added. "He's a Templar, but he lives in this part of the world. I thought it would be good if you had a local to help."

The Templar Knights had supposedly disbanded long ago, but the truth was that they still existed—in two factions. One group, led by Armand, was dedicated to protecting the Boards at all costs. And the other, led by Peraud, had less noble intentions and would go to any length to possess the Boards for their own evil purposes.

"Excellent idea," Simon said. "We're going to need someone familiar with the area, and it's better to work with someone already vouched for."

"I'll do all I can to help, sir," Saduj said. His voice was low and polite and . . . slightly familiar, like a voice from the shadows of my dreams. "And you, too, Miss Solitaire. I will be glad to help you both."

My stomach rolled again, and I wondered if the sensation had as much to do with Saduj as it did something I ate. I couldn't help staring at him, trying to figure out where I'd seen him before.

"How was your flight over?" Armand asked as he led the way through the teeming airport.

"Long," Simon said, "but Jenna insisted that we travel first class, so it was more comfortable than I'm used to." He glanced at me, then stopped walking. "Are you feeling all right? You look a little pale."

Yeah, at your condescending attitude, I thought. On the

plane he had said he'd chosen our seats for comfort on the flight, but now he was making it look like I couldn't even travel well.

"I *am* a bit queasy," I had to admit. "My stomach is doing rolls."

Simon was scanning the hallway, looking for the customs section. I glanced at Saduj, and thought I saw a disapproving look cross his face as he watched Simon.

"You need to get your land legs back," Armand said. "If you've never flown that far before, it can be a little unsettling."

My stomach did another roll, and I gulped for air. "A little?" I asked.

"Maybe we should get Miss Solitaire to the hotel," Saduj suggested. "She does not look at all well."

"Agreed," Simon said. He took my arm on one side, and Armand grasped the other while Saduj carried the luggage. "Maybe it was something she ate on the plane?"

"Maybe," Armand said. "But you aren't feeling sick, are you?"

Simon shook his head. "No, I feel just fine."

"I'll be all right," I murmured, feeling like my stomach was still back in the windstorm. "I just need to get my land legs back like Armand said."

Between them, they managed to get me through the incredibly long customs procedure, out of the airport, and into the waiting sedan. Saduj climbed into the driver's seat, while Simon and Armand sat on either side of me in the back.

The inside of the car was stifling, the air hot and dead. I'd never felt an illness come on so quickly, and the heat did nothing to help my nausea.

"Could someone open a window, please?" I asked.

"I will turn on the air conditioning in a moment, Miss Solitaire," Saduj said, his eyes meeting mine in the rearview mirror. "It is better not to open the windows. The air outside is even hotter than in here."

I felt feverish and weak. "How far to the hotel?" I asked. "I think I need to lie down."

"It's not far, Jenna," Armand said. "Quickly, Saduj."

"Yes, sir." I heard him step on the gas and turn on the air conditioner, but the faint breeze of cool air did little to help my nausea.

I closed my eyes, and tried not to throw up.

Somehow, despite the heat and my rolling stomach, I made it all the way to our hotel without throwing up all over the sedan's leather interior. Or on Simon and Armand, for that matter. The two of them managed to get me into the hotel, which felt much cooler.

I felt sweat drying on my forehead and tried to stand on my own, but immediately swayed again. Simon caught my arm and held me while Armand checked us in.

"Water," I said to Simon. "Can I please have a glass of water?"

"Sure, Jenna," Simon said. "As soon as we get to the room."

"Thanks," I said, relieved that at least they had drinkable water here.

"Excuse me, sir," Saduj said, "but it would be best to get her to her room now. She looks, I think, even worse."

"She does?" Simon asked. "I thought she sounded a little better."

"She's cooler," Saduj said, "but it won't last for long."

Another wave of nausea swept over me and I felt my body temperature rise as Saduj placed a cool hand on my forehead. "She has a fever," he said. "She needs to rest now."

"He's—right," I said, hearing the faint slur in my words. "I could use a nap." I felt my stomach twist again. "Or a bathroom."

"Uh-oh," Simon muttered.

I looked at him and saw the worry there and knew he would take care of me. I tottered toward the stairs in the direction the porter had carried our luggage, but the sight of them was too much. I didn't think climbing them was an option.

Another wave of heat wracked my body and a spasm shook my stomach. Clenching my teeth in a desperate effort not to get violently ill, I suddenly felt myself lifted off the ground. A distant voice said, "I'll just carry her," and I wondered who was coming to my rescue—Simon or Saduj?

Another voice said, "I will find a physician to see to her."

And then I passed out.

The water is rising above my head and I can no longer hear the screams of the dying. The taste of salt fills my mouth and I know that I am going to die.

I focus on memory. The touch of my lover's hand. The sound of his voice caressing my ear as we sink together into the shadows of our tent in the desert. He is dead now, too, but soon we will be together again.

Seconds pass, minutes . . . and I know that only my use of the Board of Water is what is sustaining my life. But the Board has deserted me. I lift it in my hands, the weight of the water slowing my movements.

It is pretty beneath the water, and though I can no longer hear it, I do not mourn its loss.

I wedge it into the rocks, wondering if one day another Holder will come and find it . . . or perhaps the Keeper of the Boards herself will be the one to retrieve it from this place.

I try to remember my lover again. Killed by the same men who hunted me. But I have avenged him . . . I have avenged us both.

I heard unfamiliar voices and tried to wake from my dreams. Why I kept seeing the woman hiding the Board of Water I didn't know, but I heard the Board calling to me, calling to the Board of Air, begging to be found—and used—once more.

DON'T MISS ANY OF THE BOOKS IN THE
DAUGHTER OF DESTINY SERIES:

Coming April 2006

*My name is Jenna Solitaire—
and I am the Keeper of the
Boards. I have the Board of Air.
And every day, I hear the voice
of the Board of Water calling to
me. Somehow, I must find it
and master its powers—before
someone else does....*

Having mastered the power of the Board of Air, Jenna travels
to Jerusalem to find the Board of Water. She is accompanied
by Simon Monk, who seeks the Boards on behalf of the Vatican. Jenna doesn't trust Simon, but he's her only source of information about the Boards. In Jerusalem, Jenna meets Saduj,
a local guide who claims to know the whereabouts of the
Board of Water. Simon is suspicious, but Jenna finds herself
strangely attracted to Saduj. Jenna must find the Board before
it awakens and causes unimaginable destruction. But will she
lose her heart—and possibly her life—in the process?

Coming June 2006

My name is Jenna Solitaire, and I am the Keeper of the Boards. With the elements of Air and Water at my command, I now go in search for the most dangerous Board I have sought so far—the Board of Fire.

From the searing desert of the Middle East, Jenna and Simon travel to the ancient city of Pompeii, following the clues to the hiding place of the Board of Fire—also known as the Board of the Flames. But Peraud is hot on their trail, and is more determined than ever to claim the two Boards the Keeper already possesses. Jenna must also content with her growing attraction to Simon, who is torn by his desire for her—and his sacred duty to the Church.

Coming October 2006

The whisper of Air. The power of Water. The heat of Flame. I, Jenna Solitaire, have found three of the four Boards of the Elements, but each has exacted a price. Now, I journey to England to seek the fourth Board, which can control the very Earth itself— and may also hold the key to a prize beyond imagining....

Having found the Board of Fire, Jenna and Simon hurry to decipher the clues that will lead them to the Board of Earth—and mastery over the very land itself. On their way to locate the tomb of a mythical English hero, and fending off shadowy new attackers who want the Boards for themselves, an offer of help comes from a relentless enemy. Can Jenna and Simon trust him to help them—or are they walking straight into a trap set by the one who has coveted the Boards for millennia?